D0313177

THE KING OF THE WHITE ELEPHANT
by PRIDI   BANOMYONG

11 MAY 2000

Committees on the Project for the National Celebration on
the Occasion of the Centennial Anniversary of
Pridi Banomyong, Senior Statesman (private sector)

To celebrate the centennial anniversary of Pridi Banomyong
(11 May 1900 - 11 May 2000)

Series to commemorate the centennial anniversary of the birth of Pridi Banomyong, Senior Statesman

THE KING OF THE WHITE ELEPHANT
by PRIDI BANOMYONG

ISBN : 974-7449-22-6

First English edition 1941
Second English edition 1990
Third English edition 1999, 1,000 copies

Publisher : Committees on the Project for the National Celebration
on the Occasion of the Centennial Anniversary of
Pridi Banomyong, Senior Statesman (private sector)
E-mail : Pridi@ffc.or.th http://www.pridi.or.th

Printed at Ruankaew Printing House, Bangkok, Thailand (Siam)

290 Baht

Distributed by Suksit Siam
113-115 Fuangnakorn Rd., Bangkok 10200, Thailand (Siam)
Fax : 662-222-5188

Foreward to the Third Edition

Pridi Banomyong wrote *The King of the White Elephant* during his fifteen year involvement in national and international politics between 1932 and 1947. Although Pridi was not a prolific writer, *The King of the White Elephant* stands out from his other works because it is presented in the form of a novel.

Writing a single novel may not have placed Pridi Banomyong among the ranks of professional novelists, just as directing one movie did not make him a famous movie director. Nevertheless, the classic feature of *The King of the White Elephant* lies in the fact that this work was not written by a professional novelist, but it was written by a statesman. One who wanted to portray to the world how a small country viewed peace through literature and film. The original manuscript of this novel was written in English and the movie was made with an English soundtrack.

Both the novel and the film were made in 1940 amidst the war that had erupted in Europe in 1938. The initial victory of the Axis powers lead to the exposure of Nazi-Facist ideology to Asia.

As for Siam, which had already changed its name to Thailand, the head of government and some members of the cabinet became sympathetic to the ideology of the Axis powers. Consequently, sentiments of extreme nationalism and militarism spread throughout Thai society.

Pridi tried to resist the wave of militarism in every way possible in his capacity as a member of the government. For instance, founder of Thammasat University. Pridi unsuccessfully attempted to discourage Buddhist and political studies students from organizing a protest calling for the return of land in Indochina from France. In addition, he also pushed for the adoption of the Neutrality Act of 1939.

The King of the White Elephant is another attempt to attain the goals of neutrality and peace at both the national and international level. This historical novel does not only reflect Pridi's views on peace, but it clearly portrays his views on "war and peace" which are two side of the same coin. Naturally, Pridi desired peace or the absence of war as he had concluded at the end of the novel that *'n' atthi santiparan sukhan* or "peace is the highest level of happiness for humans."

But when war is unavoidable, Pridi's position is clearly stated in this novel. That is, one must resist the aggressors to the very end. He still believed in a "just war," but at the same time he tries to limit the effects of the war so it will not affect the people, regardless of which country they belonged to Pridi believed that every person loved life, wants peace, and that war resulted from the actions of a small group of leaders who want power.

Therefore, when the European war spread to the Asia-Pacific region and became World War II, Thai military leaders allied the government with the Axis powers which had started the invasion. When Pridi was forced to leave the government and become the Regent, he fulfilled his objectives as outlined in the first chapter of *The King of the White Elephant* - the Thai Kingdom meant the land of the free. That is, Pridi, under the pseudonym "Ruth" (which came from "truth"), became the driving force behind the underground movement for peace and the liberation of the country called "The Serithai Movement." The Serithai Movement joined forces with the Allied powers against the Axis powers.

In the end, it was apparent ot the Allied powers that the Serithai Movement represented the peaceful intentions of the Thai people. Not only did Thailand emerge on the side of the victors but she also played an important role in bringing about world peace as evidenced by the proclamation of the Declaration of Peace on August 16, 1945 made by the Thai government under the royal auspices of His Majesty King Ananda Mahidol.

Even though *The King of the White Elephant* was written 60 years ago, as long as there are problems and wars at the regional and global level, the author's progressive concept of war and peace still hold true today.

Project to produce media materials, for children and youths, in honour of Pridi Banomyong, Senior Statesman

Foreward

"The King of the White Elephant" was the first and only "novel" ever written by the late Senior Statesman Pridi Banomyong. It was perhaps the first Thai novel written in English.

Pridi was not a novelist and besides, he was very busy with many affairs of great responsibility to the nation. Nevertheless, he yet found time that he had little to spare writing the historical novel of vivid imagination.

He evidently did not write it for the sake of personal enjoyment, but rather for the purpose of advocating his noble concept on peace. To the Senior Statesman, peace was a rarity to be acquired through a "just war". He made this point clear in some keywords in his novel, for example, "We do not fight against the people of Hongsa, but rather against aggression", and ending the story with the Buddhist teaching "no happiness equal to peace".

Pridi wrote the novel while he was the Finance Minister during 1939-1940 after his trip around the world in 1935 which prompted him to engineer the proclamation of Thailand's Neutrality Act. *"The King of the White Elephant"* carried his warning message of the imminent danger of another World War and of the imperative preparedness for encountering aggression. He chose English to convey his message to the Thai elites and other leaders in the region.

Both the writing of the story and the production of the film were complete in less than a year. *"The King of the White Elephant"* with original English sound - track was distributed both in Thailand and in some Southeast Asian countries just before the Pacific War broke out.

It is a blessing that the Thammasat Association of Los Angeles undertakes to publish the novel both in its original English and in its Thai translation as part of the celebration of the forty-fifth anniversary of the Peace Declaration Day on August 16, 1945. The Peace Declaration was promulgated by Regent Pridi Banomyong in the name of His Majesty King Ananda Mahidol to nullify Thailand's involvement in the Second World War.

On behalf of the Pridi Banomyong Foundation, I wish to express my deep and sincere appreciation to the valuable effort of the Thammasat Association of Los Angeles. Such effort will certainly make the celebration at Thammasat University on August 16 this year more meaningful and truly memorable.

Phornsuk Banomyong.

BANGKOK
May, 1990

Preface

This novel is based upon certain well-known episodes in the history of Thailand : the invasion of the country by her neighbour, ostensibly with the object of securing a few white elephants, but in reality for the purpose of personal aggrandizement ; the defeat in single combat of the ambitious and aggressive ruler by the greatest and noblest of Thai warriors ; the decisive victory of Right over Might ; and the exercise of that spirit of charity and compassion embodied in the teachings of the Enlightened Lord Buddha, whose noble words, uttered over two thousand four hundred years ago, still stand to-day as a kindly light towards which humanity must strive if it is to be saved from destruction.

It is the story of the olden days of the East, when nations rose up in arms at the mere word of their King, for what cause they knew not, except that they had been ordered to. Nations that today, with the enlightenment bestowed on them by the Lord Buddha, have realised the follies of their forefathers, and forgiving and forgetting, have, aggressed and aggressor, victor and vanquished alike, joined hands in brotherly love to work for the commonwealth of Mankind.

In the main it is the story of a King who ruled over Ayodaya 400 years ago. He defended his realm with his own sword and risked his life for his countrymen. In this land where elephants abound, the White Elephant is esteemed the most noble of all and so the people acclaimed their chivalrous Monarch *"King of the White Elephant."* His name was Chakra. He had no love for the vanities of his court but gave himself ·holly to the welfare of his Nation. He fought bravely but he loved Peace, and to **PEACE** this story is dedicated, for "Peace hath her victories no less renowned than war."

Pridi Banomyong

BANGKOK
11 MAY 1940

The King of the White Elephant, the first and only novel written by Pridi Banomyong
and the first Thai novel ever written in English

The film crews of *The King of the White Elephant*.
Pridi Banomyong, director (standing center holding a walking stick)

The house where Pridi Banomyong and Thanpuying Phoonsuk Banomyong stayed in during the filming of the movie in Prae province, May 1940 (BE 2483).

The director pays respect to the guardian spirits before the filming of the movie begins.

The production team of *The King of the White Elephant*.

King Chakra, ruler of the Kingdom of Ayodaya,
enters the Throne Hall to watch the dance performance.

Renoo
the Lord Chamberlain's
daughter, dances for
King Chakra.

Behind the scenes
during filming
in the Throne Hall.

King Chakra
prepares for
the elephant
hunt.

The captured elephants are rounded into the kraal along with a white elephant.

The King of Honsa enjoys
the company of his attendants.

Behind the scenes during
filming in King Honsa's
palace.

King Honsa sends an envoy to the
Kingdom of Ayodaya to ask King
Chakra for the white elephant.

King Honsa announces the reasons for going to war against the Kingdom of Ayodaya.

The People of Honsa tremble with fear upon hearing King Honsa's decision to declare war on the Kingdom of Ayodaya.

An old man who disagrees with King Honsa's decision to use violence is killed.

Behind the scenes and the production
process of the movie. Most of the
movie was filmed in Prae province
and the Thai Film Studio at Thung
Mahamake, Bangkok, owned by
Maj. Gen. H.R.H. Prince
Bhanubhandyukala

Phra Chen Duriyanga composed and arranged the song Sri Ayodaya for The King of the White Elephant. Pridi Banomyong came across this song in a French book written by Laloubère.

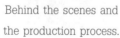

Behind the scenes and the production process.

The Honsa army prepares to attack Kanburi.

The soldiers and the people of Kanburi try their best to defend the city walls but they can not defeat the Honsa army.

The two sides engage in combat.

The Governor of
Kanburi leads his army
against the enemy and is
killed during the battle.

The victorious King of Honsa
orders his men to burn Kanburi
to the ground.

The Honsa army marches
through Kanburi.

"We are fighting against aggression. Remember!
We fight not against the people of Honsa, but against their Ruler........."

King Chakra leads his
army against the attackers.

The Ayodaya elephant army.

The Honsa elephant army.

The two armies fight one another.

The two armies fight one another.

Behind the scenes as the two armies take a break.

Most of the actors playing the role of soldiers are preparatory school students and teachers from the University of Moral and Political Sciences (now known as Thammasat University),Class 1-3 and villagers from Prae province. These actors, as well as acting directors, and photographers, willing volunteered their time and were not paid.

The fight on elephant back between King Chakra and King Honsa.

Behind the scenes while filming the fight on elephant back scene.

King Honsa is struck by King Chakra and falls to the ground.

(Picture above) After his victory, King Chakra leads his army back to Ayodaya.

(Picture below) Behind the scenes while filming scenes in the Royal Palace.

The people, ministers and faithful servants wait for King Chakra's arrival and pay their respects.

King Chakra chooses Renoo to be his first wife and then appoints her to be the Queen.

'n' atthi santiparan sukhan - There is no bliss surpassing Peace

CHAPTER I

THE OLD KINGDOM OF AYODAYA

Our story takes place in the capital of The Thai Kingdom, Ayodaya, in the year A.D. 1540 during the reign of the young King Chakra.

The Kingdom of the "Free People" is what The Kingdom of The "Thai" means. They had migrated, these keen apostles of individual and national liberty, from the far off mountains of Yunnan, driven, probably, by the Chinese invasions which spread gradually from North to South. They remained for a century at Sukhoday, then advanced again towards the Gulf of Thailand which forms the southern border of the Indo-Chinese Peninsula.

A free state had come into being, of monarchic and absolute form, but limited by the traditional benevolence of the Kings and by the tolerance and mutual aid taught by the religion of the Lord Buddha, and supported by a pervading sentiment of national independence.

Ayodaya is an old Pali word which means the absence of war, Peace--a wish and a symbol which was not realised; for the city, after many vicissitudes of fortune, was finally destroyed by the Burmese King in A.D. 1768.

The Capital, it is said, was founded in or about the year A.D. 1350 by King Phra Chao Uthong at the junction where the Mae Sak meets the Maenam Chao Phraya, the largest river

of the Kingdom which flows towards the South emptying itself into the China Sea. Far away appeared the artificial hill
of Phu Khao Thong, the golden mount, erected by ancient
tradition in every important town situated in the open plains.

The City was situated on a fortified island and, in it interior, the royal residence itself was protected by a wall which
also likewise protected, according to the practice of peoples
of Mongolian race, ministries, public offices, temples, etc......
Outside the City were quarters reserved for the inhabitants of
foreign nationality.

The two rivers were the principal means of communication for the citizens. They moved on them day and night on
their small boats which, though seemingly unstable were yet
overloaded with fruits, betel nuts, salted fish, cloths and even
furniture. They passed slowly up and down and across one
another's path without accident, skilfully propelled by their
oarsmen.

The houses, floating dwellings which appeared like large
structures on pontoons, and the markets, where confused murmurs rose to the sky, crowded the edges of these waters which
flowed past them. There were no quays; for the river-side
residents were the proprietors of the ground opposite their
floating houses; connection with the land being afforded by
emergency flying-bridges, which were hemmed in by the
"sampans" (pirogues) lying so close together that one would
have imagined that they must collide. He who wanted to
cross the river chose one, the oarsman of which, well set in
the stern, appeared deserving of his confidence; sometimes
he clambered over several boats already overloaded, and their
motion threatened to make him lose his balance. But as
everyone in this part of the world living near water knows
how to swim from tender childhood, there was no apprehen-

sion, and a fall only raised a laugh.

Ayodaya was a city of great fame. To the traveller who arrived from China by the mountainous paths of the North; to the stranger who came from India through the dreaded forests of the West; to the European, sometimes lost in these remote parts of the world after many days of travel, who came to sell the latest fascinating inventions of the West, it presented an aspect of magnificent splendour and unequalled wealth.

The palaces, the wats (temples) were inlaid with glittering materials which twinkled in the bright sunshine like jewels in fairyland. There were roads straight and well maintained, which ran by the side of the many canals or passed over them by means of bridges. And all around spread fertile fields and paddy-land, well watered by the Maenam flowing towards the Gulf of Thailand.

At long intervals, the big gabled roofs, extended by the curved antennae, the characteristic roofing of Far-Eastern Asia which originated in Burma and Sumatra, replaced the sober Greek lines and the copious curves of India.

The sun brightened the gilded and multicoloured glass with which the doors and the windows of the temples were ornamented. The buildings were tall and shapely and the monumental doors were wide enough to allow the crowd to pass through in haste on those festival days when they brought their offerings to the Lord Buddha.

Vihar Mongkol was the most sacred temple, the one where King Chakra liked to worship. Its roofing was supported by high wooden pillars lacquered in red and decorated with gold. Every wall was covered with frescoes; the doors were framed and crowned with sculptures; the panels of the windows, gilded on black lacquer, reproduced the divine beings, good or evil, who are believed to inhabit the heavens.

In the centre, gigantic and looking like a block of gold, a Statue of Buddha reigned supreme. The Enlightened Lord, the possessor of the highest wisdom, dominated with His thoughtful and benevolent smile the faithful and prostrate worshippers; and it was in front of Him that the Sovereign himself used to come to lay down his offerings and formulate his desires.

CHAPTER II
THE YOUNG KING CHAKRA

It was the middle of the sixteenth century, the time when, in Europe, three Sovereigns equally brilliant and equally selfish, the French King Francois I, the German King Charles-Quint, and the English King Henry VIII, struggled to establish their supremacy in the European world. Educated people were deeply troubled by the Reformation already in full swing, Calvin had established himself at Geneva in 1536 and Luther had died in 1540, and the gloomy clouds announced the wars of religion which would soon overwhelm these intolerant countries. In the meantime great navigators hastened to the discovery, soon to the conquest, of new lands, initiating an expansion and extension of Aryan influence in Asia, Africa, America, and the South Sea Islands, an influence destined to be checked only four centuries later. In the Far-East, it was the Portuguese flag which dominated the seas by its brilliant but fragile supremacy. Magellan had just gone to the Philippines where he subsequently met his death and Albuquerque had established himself at Malacca as early as 1515.

The young King Chakra, known to History under the name of Mahha Chakraphatr, presents a character quite extraordinary in Thai History and deserves to be studied. Brought up by an old priest in the temple, he showed a remarkable aptitude for religious studies and adapted himself to every one of the most painful necessities of the novitiate.

When he came to the Throne, after the premature death of his father, the ceremonies and the splendours of the court were disagreeable to him, and he did not fail to use his simple and severe tastes. A kind of Reformation was set in motion by the chief of the Thai State in its proper sphere at the epoch when similar aspirations were beginning to appear in the West.

CHAPTER III
A CUSTOM TO BE OBSERVED

On this day, the anniversary of the Royal Coronation, tradition makes it a day of official ceremonies and of public rejoicing.

From the morning, a crowd of officials and courtiers hasten towards the Palace to pay their homage and offer their best wishes to the Monarch. The gates are wide open, the soldiers lined up through the courtyards, with a gilded spear and shield in their hands.

Each wears the gala uniform suited to his rank: the precious cloths, brocaded with gold and silver, the helmet with a shining point, the gown with flower-designs woven in golden threads, the broadsword of ceremony with its flashing sheath and a hilt-guard decorated with precious stones. And waiting for the solemn ceremony, all stand in the Grand Throne Hall and await the propitious moment determined by the priests for the performance of the usual rites.

The Throne Hall, the place most revered, where His Majesty will appear in all solemn attire, is high and supported by ornamented columns.

The spacious hall has sufficient room to hold easily every courtier gathered therein. The girders of its roof are worked and lacquered in red. On the walls are frescoes representing religious or sacred scenes.

The waiting continues, then, suddenly, the sound of the conches breaks through the air, supported by the rolling sound of the drums. In the courtyards, the soldiers present arms at the word of command. The Master of Ceremonies knocks three times on the ground with his long rod and announces the King.

Chakra, followed by his body-guards, makes his appearance and stops one moment on the threshold to look at those who wait for him.

He is a man of noble bearing, skilled in the use of his weapons. His appearance is pleasing, robust and vigorous. His keen eyes know what to read in those of his interlocutor.

He is already renowned for the wisdom of his commands. He knows how to express his thoughts in clear and accurate terms and his instructions are neither vague nor hazy. All those who approach him receive from his presence an impression of security and confidence.

At this moment he is robed in all the glory of his royal attire. On his head rests the Mahha Mongkut (Great Crown). He is dressed in resplendent cloths and a gown of brocade reaches down to his ankles.

He moves forward slowly between rows of bowing courtiers, throwing to this one or to that one a kind look, and reaches the gilded Throne on which he seats himself to watch the ceremony. On his left is another Throne which yet remains vacant; it is the one for the First Queen, still to be designated, King Chakra not having renounced his bachelor life since his accession to the Throne.

The King is seated and the Princess of the blood take their place on one side, the Ministers and Counsellors on the other.

Now the Lord Chamberlain moves forward, a courtier

versed in the rites of the court. It is his duty to give the signal for the ceremonies and to look after their traditional routine. He is the living trustee of ancient custom. He cherishes them, he recalls them to the young and unmindful monarch. It is his duty; but it is a duty which he accomplishes by putting in the whole heart of the traditionalist steeped in the past.

Thus no one is surprised when, after having expressed the respectful wishes of the nobles and the people on this solemn day, the Lord Chamberlain adds, in a tone less official, but at the same time convincing and firm:

"May it please Your Majesty, I hope to be able today to go to the people and tell them the good news that you have followed the custom of your forefathers. The people will, I feel sure, be very glad; for it is three years now since Your Majesty ascended the Throne and Your Majesty has not yet observed the custom of your ancestors."

"What custom are you referring to?" asks the King.

"The custom that a King takes to himself three hundred and sixty five wives."

"Is not that too many?" says the King.

"No! not too many, Your Majesty. The King of Honsa, your neighbour, has broken the record. He has three hundred and sixty six."

"Three hundred and sixty six! But there are at the most only three hundred and sixty five days in a year?"

"The King of Honsa is a very clever man. All he does is to raise his first wife to the position of an honorary queen and give her a separate palace with a large pension thrown in."

"You seem to be well up in these customs," remarks the King. Cannot you find me some way to get round this custom somehow, so that I do not have to take any wives at all?"

"Impossible, Your Majesty. Impossible! The question of

wives cannot be altered. It would be against immemorial custom and there would be a general strike among the girls. Even now the eunuchs, who look after the royal harem, are threatening to strike."

"Oh!..................why?"

"Because they complain that they have no work to do, as their apartments are all empty."

The Lord Chamberlain sighs and continues:

"If you do not want the three hundred and sixty five wives all at once, you can choose one first. Only do not let the Throne be vacant. I have taken the liberty of bringing the daughters of our nobilities for Your Majesty's selection. They will dance before you and Your Majesty may select according to your taste. I implore Your Majesty for the sake of the peace of the country."

"All right," says the King, "for the sake of peace, bring them in."

"Ah!" exclaims the Lord Chamberlain, delighted. "Now Your Majesty is really wise. I am going to present to your Majesty many, many beautiful girls. My daughter is coming too. She is very, very beautiful. I recommend her especially to Your Majesty."

"My dear Lord Chamberlain," says the King absent-mindedly. "I shall be pleased to see the dance......but I do not promise that I shall follow the custom."

The Lord Chamberlain sighs. This lack of enthusiasm hurts him. During his young days........But he makes the conventional sign.

The curtain of a door opens on the left and there appears a young beauty of fifteen years. With her graceful features, her slender and flexible neck, her shoulders with flawless fall and with the beauty and flexibility of her articulations, she is, this young girl with black eyes and black hair, of the true Thai type: she belongs to the race of women who have always astonished and delighted travellers, surprised to find in this country the rare silhouettes of the Tanagras or the fascinating girls who once populated the Islands of the South Seas up to Tahiti and to the Hawaian Archipelago.

Behind her, who will lead the dances, assemble together her companions, smiling and attentive.

The dancers have been chosen from the girls whose faces are of a regular oval shape, the hair supple under the traditional diadem, the eyes wide-awake, the bust flexible, the arms so skilfully trained since childhood that they can attain all sorts of postures ordinarily impossible.

They are draped with precious cloths, silks glittering in the light with the spangles of the belts and ornamented wristbands.

They are clever in drawing complicated figures in their dance, ballerinas versed in their art, and their evolutions create an ensemble which forms and dissolves in moving lines, to the great pleasure of the enthusiastic audience.

But the Lord Chamberlain now approaches the Throne, leading the first dancer by the hand.

"Ahem! Ahem!"

"What!" says the King who was deep in his thoughts.

"As you have ordered, Your Majesty! The girls are here. Is it your pleasure that they should dance now?"

"Yes! Yes! By all means."

The Lord Chamberlain smiles ingratiatingly.

"Here is my daughter, Sire........Your Majesty! Here is my daughter, Renoo."

"So this is your daughter," says King Chakra. "Yes!..... Yes!..... very beautiful. Now let us see you dance."

The beautiful Renoo curtsies to the Monarch in the best manner of the court, so well rhythmed, so supple, that she is already dancing.

"What kind of dance would you like to see, Your Majesty?" says she, in a voice touched with emotion.

"Any dance will do. Just--er--dance," replies the King.

Renoo joins her hands together in the ritual gesture, the palms close together, the fingers with tapering nails so bent as to form a graceful curve, so bent that one would think that they would touch the back of her hands.

The orchestra, which consists for the greater part of xylophones and drums of solemn sound, plays a dance-air in quick time. The music underlines in sordine the gesture of the dancer. Renoo continues her graceful evolution according to the best traditional rhythms, supple as a bamboo shoot, her slender long-shaped arms ritually curved, her hands spreading and undulating.

Apart from the music and the dance there is only silence and heat; but the spectators are content in this heavy atmosphere of flowers and perfume which surrounds the women.

The Lord Chamberlain half closes his eyes........

Now it is that, in his dreaming heart, the vacant seat on the left of the King is filled with a human form.

He sees Renoo in occupation, the royal diadem on her forehead, smiling, resplendent.

He hears the dialogue:

"Are you happy, my dear?" said King Chakra, leaning towards the new Queen and placing his hand gently on her little one which was resting on the gilded arm of the chair.

"Terribly happy, Sire." replied Renoo. "And Father too is very, very happy. Goodmorning, Father."

"Goodmorning, Father," repeated the King. "How are

you feeling this morning?"

And dropping out totally from the realities of this world the Lord Chamberlain repeats, sotto voce, his body leaning forward:

"Goodmorning, Sire. I am feeling fine. Fine! Sire...."

His neighbour, the War Minister, cannot believe his ears. Why does the Lord Chamberlain speak to himself during the royal audience! Has he become mad? And with a nudge of the elbow the Minister recalls his colleague to the proper etiquette.

"What's all that?"

The Lord Chamberlain gasps. His eyes are open again.

Alas! The royal seat is empty, and Renoo over there continues the evolutions of a dancer classically trained....And the King? The King is deep in the reading of a document, this wretched document, which was handed over to him just now and which seems to absorb all his thoughts.

He has already read it twice, his eyebrows drawn into a frown; he seems to be plunged in deep meditation apparently not so pleasant; now he is counting on his fingers.........

Oh! Yes, it was a dream, thinks the Lord Chamberlain, and what a pleasant but futile dream.

The time passes.........The dancers, following Renoo, her eyes nearly wet with tears by the Royal indifference, retrace their way to the apartments where they will change their dress and sparkling head-gear.

The King places his hand on his forehead, and seems too, to have awakened from a dream.

He is surprised.

"Hallo! Where have all the girls gone to? Is this a strike?" The courtiers smile.

"It is, Your Majesty! But it is not the girls who have gone

on strike. It is you, Sire, who strike against them."

King Chakra shakes his head.

It is evidently no time for joking.

His look surveys the assembly, stops at the Ministers, observes the gentlemen of the court; he is, at the same time, inquisitive, thoughtful, and decided.

All are waiting, vaguely conscious of some serious happening.

But King Chakra raises his hand; he speaks with some solemnity; and his words re-echo in the deep silence which now reigns.

"Well, we thank you, my Lord Chamberlain, for bringing the girls, but the custom will have to wait for today. We have just received an urgent report that Mogul the Great has extended his power to India and has concluded an alliance with our neighbour Honsa. Not only that, Honsa is making feverish preparations for war. Our country is in imminent danger."

The Lord Chamberlain opens his eyes wide; his features show obvious contempt.

"What danger?"

"Danger from Honsa, who with Mogul's help, may at any moment crush us within the hollow of his hand."

"But," argues the Lord Chamberlain, "Honsa is our friend."

King Chakra shakes his head energetically.

"Of what worth is friendship, when it stands in the way of ambition? Don't you see? As we are now, we are easy prey for Honsa. Our army is not strong enough yet. We have fewer horses than Honsa, and even our elephants too, are less in number than theirs. Now, instead of giving me three hundred and sixty five wives, give me an additional three hundred and sixty five elephants, and our army might stand a chance against theirs. Let the custom wait till after. What do you say? What do you say?"

The Ministers and the Counsellors have listened carefully to the royal words. They bow, they clasp their hands.

"Yes! Yes! We agree with Your Majesty."

But the Lord Chamberlain is not convinced. His face evinces disagreement. He moves to take his place among his colleagues and from there utters a dissenting opinion.

"For myself, I do not, Your Majesty. I think that if you had three hundred and sixty five wives, then took them along with you to help hunt the elephants, Your Majesty might get ten times that number of elephants."

The King shrugs his shoulders slightly.

"The majority our Counsellors are in favour of an elephant hunt first. In that case let us get ready for the hunt."

CHAPTER IV
KING CHAKRA THE PEACE-LOVER

King Chakra has retired to his private apartments.

There one sees no more the sumptuousness of the Throne Hall. Chakra, the Prince with a simple heart, does not like to live in luxury, surrounded by those perishable things which prevent one from taking a detached view of life.

What he likes to see are his glass cabinets with lacquered panels, high and narrow as are the temples themselves, made specially by the woodcarvers and the decorators of the Royal Household to contain those manuscripts which are so precious that Chakra has read and reread them many times.

The apophtegms of ancient wisdom and the teachings of the Lord Buddha are there. They speak with solemnity of the indispensable blessings of Peace, this Peace which it is the first duty of a Sovereign to assure to his subjects. They praise the respect for Right, which will always end by triumphing over Force in spite of men of evil.

Chakra ponders over the responsibilities of a monarch.

Duty towards Peace must be reconciled with the duty of safeguarding the freedom of the State in case of treacherous attack. Yes, it is a problem as old as the world: only Peace with honour is worthy of its name.

The King opens one of the glass cabinets and takes from it a manuscript.

It is the Thai version of the Ramayana. It is said that the god Malivarat had given his arbitral award restoring to Rama the wife whom the King of Ceylon, Tosakan, had stolen--an award which Tosakan disregarded, preferring to go to war, only to be finally defeated. Thus, reflects Chakra, does vain gloriousness ruin those who cannot find in themselves the strength to subject it to the imperishable rules of Right.

There is also, in this glass cabinet, tales of King Asoka, the famous Hindoo Sovereign, model of Bhuddhistic Virtes: these manuscripts embody the inscriptions that he caused to be engraved on rocks and in caves.

And Chakra reminds himself with emotion how Asoka, having invaded the Kalinga country, had been impressed to such an extent by the horrors of war that he forthwith pro-claimed its renunciation and devoted himself to the triumph of the law of the Master. It is in the footsteps of that King, faithful to the Great Wisdom (Sombati) that Chakra, undeserv-ing but full of goodwill, desires to tread, in order to exalt the moral law, the source of all happiness for man and for hu-manity.........

And, taking another familiar manuscript, Chakra reads again softly the Stanza of Kotthita:

"Whoever, serene and calm, dead to the world,

"Can utter the arcana, of wisdom, the spirit without van-ity

"Without emotion,--he get rid of evils

"As if they were leaves of the forest swept by the wind."

At this moment, a light sound is heard under the shel-tered gallery which runs around the room, permitting one to live in the open air and yet to enjoy the cool breezes because its low roofs divert the rays of the sun.

A yellow gown is outlined in the doorway, silent as a

ghost, as its wearer slides on his barefeet without making, more noise than the familiar cat.

Chakra rises his head and his face brightens with a happy smile; he recognises his favourite tutor, the **phikkhu** Asana, who, in compliance with the Rules, stands in front of him in an attitude of respect, whereas the young **luk-sis** who accompanies him and holds his round and embroidered, fan prostrates himself. And the King himself renders homage to the **"Pra"**, the Buddhist priest who represents and propagates the wisdom of the Lord.

How often did they discuss the teachings written in Pali, that old classical language so familiar to them both, in the Tripitaka (the Three Baskets). Sometimes they commented on the monastic discipline contained in the first Basket (Vinay), that discipline which **phikkhus** must obey in order to be saved from sin. Sometimes they perused in the second Basket (the Sutras) the sermons of Buddha Himself, the texts of which had been preserved by His faithful disciples. Nor, finally did they hesitate to tread in the footsteps of the Fathers of the Buddhist Church in gleaning from the third Basket (Aphitharm) the controversies of Buddhist metaphysics, as complex and rhetorical as any Greek God might have wished to see......

The King invites the **phikkhu** to take a seat with him on the mat where both sit with their legs crossed, and he heaves a long sigh.

"Happy," says he, "is the **phikkhu** who is detached from all worldly things and lives on the alms of the faithful! Happy he to whom nothing belongs and who, every day, acquires a little more of the spirit of wisdom!"

"Alas!" says Asana with an indulgent smile, "not all **phikkhus** are on the steep and narrow path which leads to the blissful state of the **Pothisatras,** those privileged beings, the essential nature of whom is a great heart full of love, stretching itself out to all living beings!"

"Can this love exist," says Chakra, "when one, such as a King, has the burden of guiding a nation, and, in particular, to defend it against enemies eager for its destruction? How can a King extend his love to all the enemies of his country? Is not that to betray his subjects?"

"The *Pothisatras*," replies the *phikkhu,* "are as those immaculate and pure flowers of the lotus which rise from the mud without having ever been blemished.[1] I have always tried by the teaching which I have given you, O King, to put under your eyes this state of felicity of the *Pothisatras,* as an example which can at the same time guide you in life and lead you to happiness. Because the Buddhas are too rare, too high, too perfect for us to aspire to be or to conceive any hope of becoming their equal!"

"Yes!" agrees Chakra thoughtfully, "a King must show to his people by his virtues, his detachment from pleasure and the perfection of his patience, that he is this flower of the lotus. He must, by some wonderful act of disinterestedness, conceived in contempt of his own life and for the welfare of his people, show them that he is worthy of being their supreme and moral Chief. I have always dreamed of accomplishing an extraordinary act of this kind....."

"Blessed be such aspirations!" says the *phikkhu* approving. "Blessed be you thrice! Such extraordinary act is always within a King's reach, as the King himself is an extraordinary being in the hierarchy of human beings. But which King knows, wants, and is able to seize the opportunity to accomplish this act?"

---

(1) Nargacuna

"I humbly believe that I would know how to take it, would want to take it, and would be able to take it," observes Chakra, "with the aid of the virtue of the Lord and the support of your precious teachings."

The *phikkhu* meditates one moment.

"An extraordinary act," says he, "can be an act of unusual courage, for the protection or for the defense of others. But it can well be an act of kindness and mercy to which the nobles have not accustomed their people. Perhaps the day will come, O King, when the opportunity will be given to you."

"May that day soon dawn," says Chakra earnestly.

"Who knows?" replies the priest thoughtfully. "Do not you know, as I do, what the Doctrine says on the chain of causes and effects? The empire of suffering is around us and we enter it through birth, which gives us existence and the unfortunate attachment which we have for it. Who knows if this chain of causes and effects does not prepare, at this very moment and without your knowledge, the occasion which will allow you to accomplish extraordinary things? Who knows of the impending arrival of the ripples launched by the stone which, yesterday, fell into the lake infinitely far away? I believe, for myself, that these ripples surround us constantly though we recognize them not........."

"How brilliant and quick is the spirit of your replies!" says the King, using the phrase of King Menander in his reply to the venerable Nargasena.[1] "Were Buddha alive, he would applaud you. I shall meditate on the deep wisdom of your words, and I always feel better after our conversations."

Chakra rises.

"If you will honour me with a few more moments of

---

(1) *Milintapanha*

your presence, O venerable Asana, you will see something of interest.......It is the fourth hour in the morning,[1] and I shall give audience to this merchant *farang*[2] who has come in his strange vessel. We can obtain from him news of countries far away."

It was a small Portuguese vessel,[3] which had arrived about four weeks previously and had sailed up the river to Ayodaya.

Chakra makes a sign to an attendant to strike the gong to indicate that the hour for the audience has arrived.

At the sound the gardens become full of people as by enchantment. Numerous dignitaries climb the staircases of the palace. The Lord Chamberlain makes his appearance, accompanied by his friend, the War Minister. Guards come to stand by the doors to prevent the entrance of intruders. Then they all settle down close together, each one at his post, to wait the kind pleasure of the King.

Chakra takes his seat on a large Throne, carved, and decorated with red lacquer and gilt, which has been placed so as to dominate, in a manner suited to the Royal Majesty, the group of counsellors. Then he makes a sign, and the Lord Chamberlain comes forward, accompanied by a foreign sailor, flanked by two or three Malay servants, carriers of presents.

He is a small and thin man with a dark oval face adorned with a rather long and tapering beard, and with a drooping moustache such as that possessed by Albuquerque and Vasco da Gama in the pictures of the time. He holds in his hand a

---

(1) *Ten o'clock in the morning*

(2) *"Farang" is the corruption of the word Franc, by which Europeans were designed in the countries of the East.*

(3) *Almelda had been appointed Viceroy of India in 1508. In 1511 he sent ships to the Moluques and fought the Sultan of Java. Later on (1518) Menezes, established in Malacca, sent Ambassadors to King of Siam.*

three-cornered hat, low and rigid, and in spite of the heat, does not omit to put on a cloak of ceremony with wide open sleeves and large cuffs stretching to the fingers.

The Portuguese, who is acquainted with local custom, makes the three regular genuflexions and orders at once the distribution of his presents. A Eurasian who had travelled with the Portuguese in the Sea of the Sunda acts as interpreter.

There are two gowns of precious cloths from India and pieces of silkgoods from Persia. Some parcels left outside prove the merchant to be a good diplomat; he had not forgotten the nobles of the Court, who will have their turn later on.

In accordance with the protocol, the King does not return thanks, but congratulates the foreigner on his fine bearing, especially after the fatigues of a long voyage and expresses the desire to hear some details of his travels.

The merchant bows:

"May it please Your Majesty!" says he. "I have come on a vessel which is going to the fortress of Malacca. We left our country in the West at the beginning of the month of March......."

"The fifth month," explains the Eurasian, alluding to the Thai lunar calendar.

"We soon had the wind against us and were compelled first to lower all our sails except one and to wait till the wind had changed its direction. This took us some days. But we saw the wind dying down while we were advancing into the warmer seas along the coast of Africa and we dropped anchor in the archipelago. The sea had been rough up to the port of the Cape, which we entered at the end of May, after a journey of about three months."

"I see," says the King, "it is the extreme South of Africa."

"Exactly, Sire. We took one full week's rest. On leaving we went towards the South-East because we had to go up again afterwards to the North so as to reach the Island of Java without passing through the Straits of Malacca, which are terrible for sailors. The sea was really calm at first, but we had not to wait much longer for the ship to roll badly as the wind became violent. We had to contend with nearly one month of that weather. And we had to be very patient in order to catch the wind from the West when it became necessary for us. Six weeks after our departure from the Cape, the air became tepid and we understood that we had approached the tropical Islands."

"You never met any vessel during all that time?" asks the King.

"Very rarely, Your Majesty," replies the navigator. "There were some in the port of the Cape; but for the rest of the journey, it was principally while approaching the Islands that we met some Malay boats and two or three junks from China. In these latitudes, there were plenty of those boats called frigates which met us once we were in view of Java, nearly two months after our departure from the Cape. From there, I proceeded to the Portuguese establishments where I ran a business for one year before taking, at the port of Malacca, the boat which has brought me to the State of Your Majesty."

King Chakra nods approval.

"It would mean," he remarks, "that it must take about half a year to come from your country to ours."

"About that, Sire!"

"You, *Farangs,* are an enterprising people. We have heard about attacks delivered in neighbouring countries by the Portuguese during these last few years. Are *Farang* people fighting between themselves with the same eagerness?"

"I think, Sire," says the merchant, "that they are very bellicose. There was, in the last century, a war between the King of the French and the King of the English which lasted no less than one hundred years."

"So," sighs Chakra, "it is not in our country alone that this madness of war is raging. Why do these Kings fight thus and so often? Have they no pity for the suffering of their subjects? Tell me, who is the greatest among them?"

"Sire," replies the Portuguese, "the greatest of them all is certainly the King of Portugal. He has numerous trained troops and possesses innumerable warships. You see yourself that he is the only one who has undertaken to send his subjects to your country in order to promote his commerce and to assure constant relations with the inhabitants."

"It is true," observes the King.

And glancing towards the courtiers, he asks:

"Did you not know this?"

The Lord Chamberlain bows.

"Sire," says he, "can you ask the foreign Lord how many wives the King of Portugal has?"

The question is translated.

"But........only one," replies the sailor. "In Western countries, Kings have only one wife, because their religion prescribes that they may have no more. Only the Great Lord, who is also called the Sultan of the Sublime Porte, can have four wives and some concubines because the Islamic religion allows him such; the paradise of the Musulmans also contains houris with eyes of gazelles, who are promised to believers by the Koran for their future life."

"It is marvellous!" says the Lord Chamberlain. "If I had not the glorious privilege of being a Buddhist, I would like to be a Mohammedan."

The navigator proceeds with his recital.

"At the same time," continues he, "the King of Portugal, my Sovereign, promotes trading enterprises in the lands where the sun sets. Your Majesty knows, perhaps, that a way to reach India through those seas, instead of going from Europe to the East, has been discovered recently?"

"I had heard so," agrees Chakra, "but I did not believe it."

The merchant lowers his head and in a voice reserved for a confidential subject:

"Sire," says he, "I can tell you more. My father was a friend of Amerigo Vespucci, a sailor in the service of Our King, Dom Manoele, who succeeded by travelling towards the West in reaching these far away lands.[1] Amerigo Vespucci, assured him many times that in fact these lands are by no means those of India, those of Asoka. They constitute a world entirely new, immense, as great as Europe and Asia put together. So my Master, in securing rapidly the conquest of these unknown countries, now extends his empire over an entire part of the world!"

"This appears very strange," says King Chakra, glancing towards the venerable Asana.

This latter offers his reply:

"Really strange and perhaps really painful. In these far away countries, are not there free men, possessors of their land, having organised States?"

"Some exist," is the reply of the merchant. "It is said also that over there there are some powerful Kingdoms, rich in gold and in precious things. But they are or will be con-

---

(1) *The Portuguese merchant holds the former discovery of Christopher Columbus cheap. But it seems apparent that public opinion at that time did the same, as may be inferred from the fact that as from 1507 the map of WALDSEE-MUELLER had given the name of America to the lands newly discovered.*

quered by my powerful master."

"And what is the reason for depriving them of their liberty and of their properties?" asks the King.

The merchant hesitates a little:

"That is," says he, "because we want to bring them civilisation and, principally, our religion which will give them salvation. It is why my master also fights the Arabs who are ignorant of the true Faith and with whom our people have for this reason had countless wars."

Silence reigns for some time.

King Chakra exchanges a glance with the venerable Asana, who now declares in a quiet tone:

"We have learned that to be loved by the gods, as was King Priyadassi Tevanampriya the Great, it is necessary to honour every faith. Tolerance is the flower of our doctrine and of our race. It teaches us not to glorify thoughtlessly our own religion nor to despise or denigrate that of others, for such would be most improper conduct. Benevolence is indeed exalted by the Law of our Lord Buddha, because when one depreciates the religion of others, one renders ill service, not only to that religion, but also to one's own. Concord only is good and permits progress, so that all can become acquainted with the knowledge of others and listen complacently to their views."

King Chakra nods approvingly and continues:

"Tolerance is a jewel in the Crown of the Kings of Ayodaya. It imparts to us the Spirit of Peace. Because, as King Asoka the Great said in a remarkable Edict, the victories of the Law are preferable to warlike conquests. In war, men are exposed to violence, to death, to separation from other beings who are dear to them. We desire, as Asoka did, safety for all creatures, respect of life and Peace. Such indeed are the conquests of the Law, victories in which a King, loved by the gods, finds his pleasure. Such alone constitute true conquests. They alone are of value in this world as well as in the next."

With these words, the audience comes to its end.

*   *   *   *   *   *

It was the practice of King Chakra, early in the morning, while the priests are collecting alms, to proceed into the gardens of the temple Tepitarm to enjoy the fresh air before the sun rises higher in the sky.

He likes this peaceful place and is scarcely troubled by the games of the youngsters who are waiting to enter the school where the **phikkhus** teach them how to read and how to write.

His glance picks out the multiple colours of the "Chedis", the fringed point of which rises up to the sky. He admires the play of the rays of the sun on the faiences adorned by their own marquetry. All is colour well blended in the light already burning, all is harmony, all is splendour.

The King takes a seat on a stone bench shaded by a mango-tree, the branches of which are already loaded with young fruit, no bigger in this season than nuts.

The youngsters play. They run after each other, as children do in all lands. They cannot see the King, screened as he is from their view by an artificial rock from which water is contantly falling, spreading in every hour of the day a pleasant freshness.

How noisy these youngsters are today!

Here is one of them, who has made himself leader and dislikes to keep quiet. He is the noisiest; one hears only his voice.   King Chakra becomes impatient and frowns.   This amounts to indecency, in such a holy place.

He is on the verge of intervening, when he hears the reproaches of a young girl who, like him, deprecates all this noise.   Who is speaking?   The King finds that he knows the voice, so young and yet so steady, so harmonious and yet so grave.........

"Are you not ashamed" says the voice, "to make such a noise in the most sacred temple of Ayodaya?   Are you not ashamed of yourself?   Keep quiet, and come and sit near me; and I shall tell you what occurred to the tortoise who was too talkative, as it is related in the Jataka."[1]

Silence reigns as if by enchantment.   The King himself does not move, curious to know what will happen.

The harmonious voice continues:

"The Blessed One loved to say to talkative people that they will be victims of their own tongue, and that, by its fault, they will kill themselves.

There was once upon a time a King of Benares who talked all day long without allowing anyone to put in a word. His counsellors themselves were unable to explain to him their views.

Now it happened that a Pothisattra was born in Benares into a noble family; and the time came when he was ap-pointed, because of his rank and his obvious virtues, a royal counsellor.   And he was anxious to cure the King of his un-becoming habit.

One day the people, who were in the court of the palace, were greatly surprised to see a tortoise fall down from the sky and break itself with a loud noise on the ground.   Tortoises do

---

(1) *Jataka, II, VII. 5*

not have the habit of flying in the air, do they? So everyone cried out that it was a miracle, except the tortoise itself which had nothing more to say.

The King was told of this extraordinary event, and he proceeded with his counsellors to the place where the dead tortoise lay.

"This is very peculiar!" said the King. "Is it an omen? I would like someone to explain this extraordinary event. I would like to know........."

And the King proceeded on and on until the Pothisattra raised his hand indicating that he would explain, because the Pothisattras know all things and this one, furthermore, was pleased to find such an opportunity of giving a lesson to the too talkative King.

"May it please Your Majesty!" said he. "I can tell you that this tortoise lived in a pond on the slope of the Himalayas. She knew two ducks and all the three of them were good friends. One day the two ducks told the tortoise they would go to stay at a delightful place near the Golden Cave and the tortoise was deeply grieved. "Why", said the ducks, "do you not come with us?" The tortoise sighed: "Because I would need not less than some two hundred years to reach the Golden Cave." The wise ducks then made her a proposition: "Listen, tortoise, we would very much like to take you along with us; but it must be on the condition that, during the whole journey, you will not say a word to anyone." The tortoise who disliked to leave her friends promised everything. "Good!" said the ducks. And they taught the tortoise how to put a stick between her teeth; then, each duck taking one end of the stick in its bill, they all flew away through space. The beginning of the journey passed quietly. But when the trio arrived above Benares, the people of the town, who were inclined to gaze up into the sky, gathered together and told each other to look at the flying tortoise by shouting loudly: "Oh! Oh! how incredible! Two ducks are carrying a tortoise away with a stick!"   This displeased the tortoise whose tongue had been itching for a long time.   "And if my friends take me with them, how does that concern you, wretched gapers?" So said the tortoise, or rather it was what she would have said. Because, on opening her mouth, she lost hold of the stick, fell down to earth and killed herself in the court of the palace. This, O King, the **Pothisattra** concluded, is what occurs to chatterers who do not know that they should speak only at the moment when it is necessary.

The King made a slight frown; but as he was a man with a kind heart, he declared: "I believe that the wise counsellor has spoken about myself." The **Pothisattra** bowed: "Surely O King! not only for you alone; anyone who speaks for no purpose may incur the same misfortune......" And from that moment, the King of Benares learned to speak little.........."

The voice of the narrator stops one moment, and then concludes:

"O Never forget this story, children; and now it is time for you to go to school. As for me, I shall return to the house to look after the work of the servants."

King Chakra is delighted and asks himself again where he could have heard that voice before.

Now the young girl follows the central alley which leads to the monumental door of the temple. She appears, followed by two girl-servants who hold her umbrella and packages. And the King then recognises the smart silhouette with its supple and rythmic bearing.

"So it's she," says he to himself. "It is our dancer of the other day. It is Renoo, the daughter of the Lord Chamberlain.

She is, I dare say, more sensible than her own father, and she would do well to take an opportunity to tell him the Jataka story of the tortoise.........."

He smiles at his own thought and then at the graceful silhouette which disappears without seeing him; yet to look at her is a kind of pleasure that he has never yet enjoyed.

CHAPTER V
THE ELEPHANT HUNT.

All is ready for the elephant hunt.

Some weeks previously, the War Minister, who is charged with such enterprises, had said to the King:

"Sire! Over there seems a suitable place for the construction of the kraal,[1] so that soldiers can be sent into the forest to drive the elephants in."

"Make your arrangements," the King had said.

Ordinarily when a fine lonesome elephant which has been detected in a forest is to be captured a simple expedient is adopted. A female-elephant is sent to bellow in the forest; when the male hears her, he rushes forth and follows her. The traitress, who has been well trained, leads the way and brings her blind lover to a large cage which she enters first. The male follows her and the trap closes; the fierce animal is henecforth prisoner.

The captured elephant is soon reconciled to his fate. His own kind is used to tame him. He is hemmed in by two others who press against him strongly, being well acquainted with that exercise. Climbing on the back of the captive, driv-

---

(1) *Kraal is a word which seem to have been taken by the Thais from the Malay language. Some see in it a corruption of the Spanish word "corral" which indicates enclosures reserved for domestic beasts of burden and cattle.*

ers teach him to drill, with the help of an iron rod. He cannot move. His fellows set him upright with blows of their tusks if he wants to lie down. Besides, he is fasting and receives a little food only if he behaves himself in a manner proper to an elephantine gentleman.

But today, the hunt is to be on a grand scale, since it is by hundreds that the animals are to be captured. It is a memorable date in the life of the country, a date which will be spoken of for generations. And each person comes from far away either to take part in the hunt or else to take the less dangerous but almost equally exciting part of a spectator.

That is why for some weeks preparations have been made by day and by night.

When the hunters have chosen the place to which it will be easy to drive the wild elephants, they do not hesitate to go and search for them as far away as the North if necessary.

In the forest, the trees are cut down to provide an empty space. The axe falls in turn upon lofty teak trees, incorruptible and hard columns of the most noble of woods, the precious "takien", the reddish "tabeck" with elastic fibers, the "mai-yang" which when fallen spreads over the ground a resinous odour.....They all stood there, dressed in their branches up to the roof of the forest which protects its inhabitants from the burning rays of the sun; the forest in which monkeys conceal themselves, jumping from tree to tree and watching the disquieting moves of the wild animals far below.

The axe fells the venerable inhabitants of the forest. On the ground, their bark is removed; they are cut up--poles are needed in great numbers for the trap.

The tame elephants are there, helping in this task. Without effort they push with their tusks the thick logs which lie on the ground. Obediently, they push or drag them along to the appointed place.

And for the first time in years, the burning rays of the sun stretch on this clearing and spread over it a beneficent cloth of heat which dries the earth's dampness, curls the dried leaves and brings death to the mosquitoes and other bearers of germs which lodge in these feverish and obscure solitudes.

The kraal is an enclosure formed by heavy poles driven deeply into the ground, unshakable where they stand. It contains one very narrow gate through which the animals can easily enter.

In the meantime, the wild elephants are gradually driven, without themselves knowing it, towards the kraal, harassed by the hunters and the tame elephants on which they ride.

Gradually the circle narrows. The animals feel indignant at the danger they foresee and yet can no more escape than fish caught in a net. One last effort, and, surrounded on all sides, hustled, they rush through the gate which seems to be the only opening. They are caught.

There is a tumultuous uproar, since captured elephants make a great noise. They protest, by beating the ground with their trunk, against the loss of their liberty.

But they have not yet gone through the worst. When an elephant comes near the fence, the men on the watch throw out ropes which catch his legs, his neck, his tail and, with extraordinary dexterity, form a kind of saddle which will tie him up and render him powerless.

The tame elephants look on at this scene, which perhaps stir up old memories. They touch him with their trunk as if in consolation; such gestures are sometimes well, sometimes roughly, received.

The captured animal becomes desperate, and attempts to calm his fever are made by throwing on him plenty of water.

Henceforth, he will not walk unless compelled by other elephants ready to give him severe punishment. He will learn, in ten or fifteen days, that all his efforts are worth nothing and that his liberty is finally lost. He will not go to his bath unless escorted by his two vigilant guardians, one on each side, who, like many human beings, have learned to side with the strongest party; soon he will resign himself to the same fate.

But here comes the War Minister at a run.

"Sire! Sire! There is a white elephant ("Chang Phuak") among them."

"This is a miracle indeed!" exclaims King Chakra. "No white elephant has been captured for many years. What does tradition say of this?"

The War Minister replies with some solemnity:

"Our fathers have said, O Majesty, that the bodies of such pure and noble creatures are inhabited by the soul of the best of us, which, having spent generations in less noble forms to redeem their sins, have at last obtained this redemption. A white elephant can shelter only the soul of a King or of a hero. This is why these sublime animals are possessed of a remarkable wisdom, with which they benefit their happy possessor."

"And what says tradition," asks Chakra, "when it is a King who captures a white elephant?"

"Tradition," continues the Minister, "says that if a King captures a white elephant, he will reign over his people in peace; and that means that our Kingdom will not be subject to the rule of Honsa or of Mogul the Great."

"This White Elephant is sacred," declares the King in a loud voice, "and it will bring peace to the people. Henceforth let the emblem of the White Elephant be the National Flag of our country."

The hunting ends amidst clamours of enthusiasm, and everyone discusses the great presage of prosperity that the virtue of the King--of which no one is in doubt--had acquired for the country of Ayodaya.

The following day, the White Elephant, duly accompanied by the royal parasol and by the bodyguards who have been attached to him, makes his way towards the Capital. The procession, headed by musicians, attracts all the people of the country, who are struck with admiration and prostrate themselves before him.

Meanwhile the elephant, young and complaisant, seems astonished at nothing, and quickly accustomed to his novel condition, trots along, wagging his head and blinking his eyes, as if he had always belonged to the nobility accustomed to the veneration of the whole people.

He has indeed no reason to complain of his fate. The best herbage is served to him: bananas, sugar canes, rice-cakes are offered him liberally. His drinking water itself is perfumed. Never had he surmised, in the deep forest, that there were such delights to charm the taste nor that the stomach could be filled with such wonders.

He trots towards the special pavilion which has been hastily prepared for him at Ayodaya, amid the admiring exclamations of the people. He is decorated with many kinds of flowers among which dominates the perfume of "Dok Mali" (jasmine) which lulls one to sleep with its pleasing smell. There is also a whole orchestra prepared to receive him, and the goldsmiths manufacture golden chains for his use. Gilt captivity!

The White Elephant, king of the wild forests, becomes, as the result of human will, a great noble. He receives titles of nobility. He is the indisputable possessor of a magnificent red and gilded parasol which will protect him from the inclemencies of the weather. He will participate in all the great royal festivals, in sumptuous state harness, near the gate of the Royal Palace. And he will not be the least honoured in the ceremony, accepting with benevolent placidity the genu-flexions and the offerings plentifully piled up at his feet.

And now in Ayodaya, the craftsmen prepare in haste, in obedience to the command of the King, the red standard on which stands out the noble profile of the White Elephant, the standard which was to become for centuries that of the King-dom of the Thai.

CHAPTER VI
HONSA DEMANDS A WHITE ELEPHANT

In his palace, the King of Honsa lies on a low bed covered with the skins of beasts killed by him in his hunts. The King is a great hunter, a great drinker and a great admirer of the good-looking girls whom nature brings forth to adorn this world.

At this moment, the great heat of the day has just passed.

Awakened from his siesta, the King of Honsa is fanned by the day's favourites and contemplates them with a satisfied glance. His Ministers are seated around the bed waiting for the important communication for which they have been assembled.

The King of Honsa shakes his head, meditates one moment, then decides to speak:

"We have just received a reply from the Great Mogul," says the King. "He is also of our opinion. For the satisfaction of our country, Ayodaya must be destroyed."

"May it please Your Majesty," interposes the Lord Chamberlain, "there should be reasonable cause for a war. Ayodaya has no quarrel with us, and King Chakra has always been our good neighbour, I do not understand why we have to fight him."

It is not the opinion of the Prime Minister, who disposes of the difficulty to his own satisfaction by stating peremptorily:

"May it please Your Majesty! Your Majesty's command is sufficient cause."

"Your Majesty!" continues the Lord Chamberlain. "If you attack Ayodaya, you will have the whole world against you."

This causes the King of Honsa surprise; he bursts into laughter.

"The whole world? You think the whole world will form themselves into a league against me?"

"But, your Majesty," replies the Lord Chamberlain timidly, "it was only last month that you signed the Arbitration Treaty with Ayodaya."

Another burst of laughter from the King of Honsa; he turns to the Prime Minister:

"Listen to him: treaties indeed! I will show you what to do with treaties."

He points out a cupboard to one of the girls.

"Bring me the Treaty with Ayodaya!......."

When the young woman hands him the document, Honsa the King opens it and reads it quickly, grumbling:

"A Treaty of Arbitration between Honsa and Ayodaya...."

Then with an impulsive gesture:

"......Treaties!......Pooh!......"

In two, in four, in eight pieces is the document torn up by the irascible monarch and these fly in the face of the unfortunate Lord Chamberlain, who retires to the rear.

The Prime Minister finds this a good opportunity to add:

"We either fight now or never at all. I have heard news that Ayodaya has just caught a lot of elephants."

Prince Bureng intervenes:

"Not only that, Sire, Chakra has also got a white elephant. That is supposed to be a good omen for him."

"A white elephant, eh? Make your preparations now,

while we send an envoy to demand the white elephant from the King of Ayodaya. He will not give it to us, of course, and we can take his refusal as a provocation to war. You leave for Ayodaya at once and tell them that if they want to live in peace, they are to send their white elephant to us. If they refuse, we will destroy Ayodaya."

CHAPTER VII
THE ULTIMATUM

King Chakra has taken his seat in the Throne Hall.

His forehead is lined with frowns, for he is to receive Prince Bureng, Envoy Extraordinary of the King of Honsa. What does this turbulent neighbour want from him? Nothing good, to be sure!

Still, thinks King Chakra, he does honour me by sending an Envoy. The Great Mogul usually requires the Chief of the neighbouring Kingdoms to go to him and to receive his advice; and in what condition do the unfortunates come away from these interviews, shaken between the terror of dictatorial menace and the shame of surrendering thier country to the caprice of the powerful Lord.

So thinks King Chakra and his thoughts carry him to the precious words:

"Good will is a virtue most sublime."[1]

The idea cools his mind, as a vivifying stream appeases the torment of the traveller during the summer heat.

Then let him come in, this Envoy of the King of Honsa!

The Lord Chamberlain announces:

"His Royal Highness Prince Bureng, Envoy Extraordinary from Honsa."

Prince Bureng, followed by two aides-de-camp, stops one

---

(1) *Motto of the Buddha-Tharma Association of Thailand.*

moment at the threshold of the door. He observes with a critical eye the harmonious decoration of the Throne Hall, the attitude full of dignity of King Chakra.

He continues his walk, showing more haughtiness than nobility, between the two rows of courtiers, Counsellors and Ministers nearer to the Throne.

With the conventional salute Prince Bureng now begins:

"I have been entrusted with a message from my Master, the King of Honsa, Ally of Mogul the Great, the All Powerful, to ask Your Majesty for your white elephant."

King Chakra does not wince.

He looks in silence at Prince Bureng, who takes from the hand of one of the aides-de-camp the royal message wrapped in precious cloth and presents it with his hands.

The King unfolds the document; he reads it in a loud voice. The letter has the merit of brevity.

His attention had been drawn, so said the King of Honsa, to the fact that Ayodaya was making hurried preparations for war. The recent elephant hunt, during which Chakra had the audacity to capture a white elephant, was definite proof of war-like measures. Faced with such provocation, Honsa had no choice other than to denounce the Arbitration Treaty. Peace could nevertheless be still secured by the surrender of the white elephant within three days, for Honsa had no designs on the sovereignty or independence of her neighbour. However if such reasonable request were refused, Ayodaya must take the responsibility for the result.

King Chakra slowly refolds the document. He glances towards the ranks of his Counsellors. He sees them trembling furiously, with blood rising to their faces, and with their proud hands playing with the swords which hang at their sides.

They are indeed as the Monarch wants to see them. He

shifts his seat, his head shows haughtiness, his glance domineering:

"Go back and tell your Master that we regret we cannot accept his proposal of peace backed by a threat of force."

"Think well of your answer, O King!" replies the Prince. "My Master's request is very reasonable. It is merely a request for an elephant."

"What your Master asks for concerns our national honour," says Chakra in a loud voice, "for the White Elephant is an animal sacred to us. If he resorts to force to attain his ends, tell him that we shall meet force with force. You have our leave to withdraw from our presence."

CHAPTER VIII
WAR!

As the King of Honsa, in his private apartment, is in good humour and teases the day's favourites, one of them at a glance of the master runs to close the door of the hall. Heady liquors had been presented to the King and the intimate siesta passes off gaily.

From the close door the bodyguard moves off without noise, and, with ribald eyes, joins his comrades in the distant corridor.

"The King is amusing himself......."

But at this moment there arrives, in a hurry, Prince Bureng, accompanied by the Prime Minister. They exchange words rapidly and make their way towards the door of the royal apartment.

The door is closed? It is not necessary to ask why. A song can be heard from the outside. Hysterical laughs, familiar remarks can be heard..........

The two newcomers look at each other and the Prime Minister scratches his ear. He knows that the King dislikes to be disturbed when he indulges in such domestic pleasures. But Prince Bureng is less discreet.

There is a crack in this door and the Prince aplies his ear to it; but it is without great success; so by a furtive gesture, he tries to open the door a little.

He bends down the better to look into the room. More hysterical laughs, more confused murmurs. The Prime Minister can no longer curb his mounting curiousity. He taps Prince Bureng for a peep. The latter with eyes glued to the slit between the doors will not budge. He even resists the Prime Minister's more violent pushes. A struggle follows and under their combined weight the doors open, and send the two sprawling into the royal presence.

A deadly silence.

"What do you want?" thunders the King of Honsa.

They would very much want, these unfortunates, to be far away and not to have made this calamitous entry into the apartment......

But business is business.

"Prince Bureng has returned, Sire!" stammers the Prime Minister.

"I can see that" says the King sarcastically. "Well, Bureng?"

Prince Bureng retrieves his mental balance, makes the ritual salute and begins to speak:

"May it please Your Majesty, I have just returned from Ayodaya and bring you good news. King Chakra has refused your demand, Sire!"

The face of the King of Honsa lightens up.

"What did I tell you? Get your men ready, and pointing to the other, you attack with your army straightaway and prepare the way for me."

The Prime Minister bows obsequiously:

"I shall move tonight, Sire, and by tomorrow their border town will be in our hands."

"Good!" says the King.

He considers one moment: a little bit of care is suitable for winning public opinion, at a time when one launches a war; thus adding:

"And now let us go and explain the situation to our beloved people, shall we?"

While orders are being given to call forth the people to the big square in front of the Royal Palace, the King of Honsa seems to be a prey to a kind of sacred derangement: is it this that the gods send to mortals whom they want to destroy or is it a symbol of the divine mission of a conqueror?

He hardly asks himself the question: he gives the command to assemble, by a blow of the gong, the population of the Capital around the Royal Palace.

The messengers run hither and thither through all the streets of the city. The air re-echoes with the sound of the official gongs: close by, it shakes the air like the firing of a gun; further away, it verberates like a murmuring tocsin which spreads anguish and uneasiness in the heart of the women, anxious and prompt to remember so many old and bad omens.

The King of Honsa devours his impatience.

He listens to the imperious sounds, and soon, a murmur rises from the crowd which, progressively, reassembles round the palace, betraying disquiet in their anxious faces and by the glances they exchange. What disaster will again befall the country of Honsa, already exhausted by deprivation and ignorance of the happiness of life, to satisfy costly caprices?

The time has come.

The King of Honsa walks towards the Royal terrace which faces the large central plaza. Here he appears, the King. They see him reaching the balustrades, then stopping.......

The Sovereign looks at the people so assembled. Around him, his Ministers remain cheerless and silent, as they know that this people desire, above all else, a lasting Peace and do not care for conquests.......

But the Lord Chamberlain has thrice knocked on the ground with his official rod.

"Silence! Silence! His Majesty the King of Honsa!"

And the King speaks:

"My people, the King of Ayodaya has refused my generous proposal for Peace. There is no other course consistent with honour. Let each one of you make ready for war. We shall then attack Ayodaya."

The silence persists. The crowd keeps still, anxious. No acclamation salutes the words of the King. Each one looks at the other, seeing his own feeling reflected in the eyes of his neighbour.

Only a venerable old man, bent with age, but with frankness and decision in the eyes, raises himself and advance up to the foot of the royal terrace:

"May it please Your Majesty, the people are tired of wars. During my life time, I have been called over ten times to war; and what is one single White Elephant? I feel sure that what Your Majesty wants us to die for can be obtained by peaceful negotiations."

The words fall upon this unpropitious silence which precedes the storm.

In the angry face of the King of Honsa, appear irritation and stupefaction. Anger fills him as a consuming fire, liberating the impulsive gesture that dictates his natural cruelty.

The King of Honsa has no more control over himself, no more respect for human life. He throws around him murderous glances. He stretches out his arm and seizes the spear of the guard standing nearby.

As lightning the weapon flies, thrown with a trained hand; it reaches the old man, cuts through his clothing, pierces his skin, his heart. Without a sigh, the man falls. Ten wars in the service, of the King of Honsa.........

It is the first victory of the King in this war; and surely not a victory over himself, such as is taught by the Lord Buddha.......

He remains there, his arm raised in a menacing gesture.

"My command is the supreme law!"

The crowd has understood. Slowly it retires towards the shelters in the town. Proximity to the Great brings only trouble and insecurity.........Happy, thrice happy those who are forgotten and efface themselves in peaceful mediocrity! But happy, a hundred times happy those whose country enjoys the blessings of Peace! Peace secured by the wisdom and firmness of the Ruler, not by pusillanimous and dishonourable surrender, Peace with all its inestimable gifts........ Alas! Already there sounds the call of the military messengers, who summon the people to the fight! Make haste! Hurry! Do not be sleepy! Run! Over there! Assemble here!

War........................

CHAPTER IX

THE ASSAULT ON KANBURI

"**A** King is becoming when in war attire",[1] said the King of Honsa while putting on his field uniform and choosing a spear, a sword, and a shield from his most favourite weapons.

He called for his fighting elephant, and climbed, with the help of his aides-de-camp, up the side of the haughty animal, tall and solid as a house. The royal seat was carved and covered with valuable skins. On the left and on the right were those weapons of war which the King might require.......Spears, pikes, glaives, broadswords, all sparkle under the sun.

The army, commanded by the Prime Minister, had preceded the Monarch. The cavalry went in front in order to induce the infantry, massed behind it, to maintain a quicker step.

The troops crossed the jungle, following the tracks marked, at long intervals, by a water-hole or stagnant pool where the horses drank. There was no forest; nothing but bushes, through which one passed without difficulty, in spite of the ground rough and uneven because of the last rainy season.

---

(1) From *Tharmapada, Khuddaka Nikaya or Buddhist Stanza of the Section of the Khuddaka-Nikaya.*

A hill marked the horizon, at first but a blot in the sky......

It was straight to it that the Prime Minister made his way, nearer and nearer until they reached its foot and might look up its slope.

The officer who rides by the Prime Minister draws with his arm a fancied line which runs along the hillsides.

"Here is," says he, "the boundary line between our country and Ayodaya."

"Be careful of the frontier guards of Ayodaya," replies the Prime Minister.

But nothing moves in the neighbouring ground. Are they so indifferent or too sure of themselves, the people of Ayodaya?

Further on they perceive at last three guards who appear to be taking a peaceful walk, watching over the horizon without much interest.......

The officer orders four horsemen to leave their mounts, to climb silently up to the guards and to kill them unawares. And the men creep away, passing from bush to bush, from grove to grove, and approach their destination without noise, barely moving, it seems, in the torpor of this tepid and sleepy afternoon.

They are already close to the enemy. Two sentinels fall, without a chance to defend themselves.

But the third is more alert. He returns blow for blow, fells one of Honsa's soldiers, and, without delaying any further, flies as an arrow to the nearby grove where horses are hidden.

Before the men of Honsa can prevent him, the guard has jumped on to his horse and raced at full speed to Kanburi, the nearest city of his country, the loop-holed high defensive walls of which could be perceived in the distance.

Kanburi, was a typical example of towns built in that

period.

An agglomeration of houses, some, pressed close together, others separated by large spaces of land which were cultivated for the use of the family. The houses were generally of wood, sometimes of bamboo, covered with attap; and they all had a verandah open and sheltered where it was more pleasant to remain or to take one's meals during the warm hours of the day.

The gates are open.

The guard gallops his way into Kanburi. He proceeds right through to the residence of the Governor. The people move aside to allow this bewildered horseman to pass.

But there is a dense group of people in the road a few hundred years away. What luck! the man thinks, for he recognises the Governor making his daily round of the people under his jurisdiction.

The Governor, unassuming and fatherly, walks along followed by a horse from which he has dismounted, the more easily to greet the townsmen. He displays no official pride. He has taken off the gold embroidered gown and the helmet with its gold spike, insignia of his office which a servant carries simply behind him.

The arrival of this horseman disturbs this peaceful walk; for the man has stopped, out of breath, and evidently wishes to speak to the Governor.

"What is the matter?" says the latter.

"The Honsas are coming, Sir!"

"What!" exclaims the Governor.

"They crossed the border by the hill," explains the newcomer.

It is no longer a question of taking a quiet walk.

The Governor of Kanburi, far from being a young man,

has all the strength of the trained warrior.

A sign to someone to help him on with his gown and to cover his head with his helmet......now his horse.

"To arms! To arms!" shouts the gallant Governor of Kanburi galloping to the barracks.

"To arms! To arms!" repeats the excited population among whom the news spreads swift as a flash of lightning.

"To arms! To arms!" shriek the provoking trumpets with their wild notes vibrating in the air.

The first step to be taken is to close the gate of the town. One soldier pushes it without success, calls for help from volunteers to hasten the erection of this protecting barrier between the inhabitants of Kanburi and the people of Honsa.

Boom!.......Boom!.......Boom! shout the gongs with pro-longed vibrations.

Crr!..........Crr!..........Crr! groan the hinges of the solid gate violently closed in haste.

"To arms!.......To arms!........" shout the soldiers, who arrive at top speed, some with muskets, some with spears, some with pikes.

They climb the high and narrow steps of the solid ram-parts and take up their positions at the crenelles.

Yes!.........Yes!.........There they are, Honsa and his troops.

"Soldiers to your posts!" calls out the Governor who watches the ramparts. "Hurry!"

And now everyone observes the soldiers of the invader, who run, flourishing their weapons, towards the city of Kanburi.

They realize the city cannot be taken by surprise, as op-timism led them to hope; fighting will be necessary.

Already, through the crenelles of the high defensive walls, firing sounds. The shots are occasional because it is not easy to manipulate these new fangled weapons into which one must skilfully pour in the powder; besides they are liable, if one does not take care, to burst in one's hands.

The soldiers of King Chakra do their best and some well aimed shots knock down some of the enemy on the ground they have invaded................

But, in fact, they prefer hand to hand fighting, which is more consonant with the glorious tradition of olden days. The gate has been left ajar to allow the main body of the troops to rush outside the wall; and there they are, charging at the soldiers of Honsa.

The combatants soon meet; there is tumult and shouting, a vociferous and murderous scramble.

Behind the first attackers, there emerge from the bushes the cavalry and a re-inforcement of infantry which has been concealed there. With the struggle in full swing, and order is heard and now thess troops rise, rushing towards the fight.........

But against these horsemen, the riflemen on the high defensive walls direct their shots in a most efficient manner. This makes them hesitate, the horses rear at this noise. The confusion is becoming more confounded. The issue remains uncertain....Kanburi, after all, is better defended than anyone ever thought. So well defended that the Prime Minister of Honsa hesitates. He has never been very enthusiastic, in his heart, for this superfluous expedition. Has not the coup failed? Would it not be best, in any case, to refer to the Most Powerful Lord whose bellicose will has driven them into this adventure?

The affair, decidedly, has taken a wrong turn. The soldiers of Honsa hesitate, aware of resistance which they have not expected.

The Prime Minister decides:

"Hey! Retire!....Hey! Retire!....Retire!" says he to his orderly officer, "Make them retire!"

"Retire! Retire!" passes on the officer.

And the troops, gradually, retire to their prepared position in the rear. There remains on open space where one can count the dead and dying.

CHAPTER X

THE SACK OF KANBURI

The surprise-attack on Kanburi has failed.

But the Governor of the twon labours under no delusion. He knows Honsa--failure only increases that King's obstinacy and ferocity.

He calls two horsemen:

"Come here, you two!"

And gives them his instructions:

"Ride to the Capital and ask for reinforcements at once! Go!.......Go quick! Do not lose time! Our safety depends on you."

They have passed through the gates of the town, the messengers of the Governor. They look only to their goal, over there, Ayodaya, where are King Chakra and the army of the country.......

Already Kanburi is behind them. But the invaders have been careful to watch the road which stretches to Ayodaya..........A shot sounds. Then another one.......

Hit by the sharp-shooters, one after the other, the messengers of the Governor fall in heaps to the ground hardened by the heat! And their liberated horses hesitate for a moment, run wildly, then peacefully graze in the fields.

Over there, behind, at Kanburi, the Governor calculates the time which his messengers will take to reach the Capital and the time for the reinforcements to reach him.

And, on the other side of the hill which separates the States involved in the war, is the King of Honsa, seated on his war elephant and he also computes the time necessary for his advance-guard to capture Kanburi by surprise, to reduce without effort its defenders to powerlessness and to make them prisoners. It should have been done already.....Why does the time pass so slowly?...... Why?......

But there come horsemen. Ah! It is the aide-de-camp of the Prime Minister.

So all has been settled. One will know all about it. And one can, from now on, leave Kanburi, duly occupied, to step on proud Ayodaya.

But why has this officer a discomfited appearance? Why does he not advance with the haughty countenance of the victor?

The aide-de-camp has made the customary genuflexions; and, with a heart full of apprehension, he starts his miserable report:

"Sire! The Prime Minister has sent me to inform Your Majesty that we have been unable to capture Kanburi. The town was strongly defended and we have been forced to re-tire."

He has finished his report, that unfortunate aide-de-camp. And he does not dare to look up at the face of the King, who alights from the powerful and awe-inspiring royal elephant.

He does not wait long.

Is it thunder which breaks in the cloudless sky? The roar of Honsa's voice has the repercussion of thunder and his eyes are filled with flashes of anger.

"Retire?........" he shouts, as if this word strikes him with amazement. "There is no such word in my vocabulary......Go back!......To where you came from...... And tell the Prime Minister to get his troops on the walls of the town otherwise he will be beheaded!......And you too!......Go!"

The King has spoken. And feeling all shaky, the aide-de-camp makes the ritual salutation and retraces his way to the stream in the vicinity of which the Prime Minister is waiting. And these two men can no longer fail to understand that there is no other way than to conquer or to die.

At Kanburi, one knows also that it must be either victory or death. The ramparts are well guarded. But fatigue reigns supreme. Often the men drowse and the officers go round to wake them, to test the condition of their weapons.

The waiting has been long..........

But movement of troops is seen far away. Unfortunately it is not from the direction of Ayodaya whence reinforcements should come.

No. It is the soldiers of Honsa who have been reassembled; and incensed this time, it seems by a new fury, they rush towards the ramparts.

Some flourish their glaives or pikes. Others carry on their backs the ladders intended for the assault. Hooks are prepared for fastening them to the high defensive walls.

The defenders fire on these advancing troops. But the attackers have learnt to throw themselves flat on the ground to avoid the rather clumsy shots of the guns.

"Advance! Advance!" yell the officers of Honsa.

And, like a reply given in a confused uproar, one hears from far away coming from the woods which have hidden them, the rhythmed trot of horses and the heavy steps of war-elephants which appear to emerge from all sides.

This sight stupefies the defenders of Kanburi...

"Sir!" shouts the officer to the Governor from the top of

the ramparts. "The enemy arrives in great numbers, they are pressing us hard on all sides and our ammunition is nearly spent. What shall we do?"

"We have already sent to the Capital for re-inforcements," repeats the Governor with a desperate gesture. "I do not know what is delaying them...... Perhaps.........our men did not get through............."

But the soldiers of Honsa are already at the foot of the ramparts with their ladders and climbing hooks.

"Stick to it!......Stand fast!......The fate of the country depends on this fight......" he exhorts.

And to the warriors on the ramparts:

"Keep your places at all costs and be killed where you stand!"

He waves his spear desperately:

"Fight on!.....Fight on!....."

Without delay the soldiers of the town pass new weapons to the defenders on the ramparts. They shout to each other information regarding the movements of Honsa's troops.

The assault continues uninterrupted.

The attackers raise their ladders on to the high wall. The defenders are able to hurl back some which, loaded with besiegers, fall heavily to the ground amid yells and cries of pain.

But more ladders are brought. They are moving, so it seems under the bunches of besiegers who climb them. The first comer falls pierced by a spear thrust.........The second comes to grips. The third takes advantage of this struggle to step on to the wall.......

Inferior in number, the troops of Kanburi are overwhelmed, driven back.

Now the ramparts are crowded with Honsa's men.....They hustle the defenders out and drive them to the foot of the high walls inside the town......

They follow them there too, striking the weary defenders relentlessly. The struggle now takes place in front of the first houses of the town..........

The Governor is one of the first to fall, run through with a spear, after having killed two attackers with his own hands.

The fate of Kanburi has been decided.

On the ramparts, Honsa's troops shout out cries of victory. They signal to the troops stationed outside, with the elephants excited by this tumult, moving their heavy legs rhythmically and trumpeting noisily.

It is now for the elephants to play their part in the struggle.

It is not necessary to excite them much. They move off......Here is the strongest, a bulky but nimble colossus, moving straight towards the gates of the town.

Solid and heavy in teak bound with iron, still closed as a last but vain obstacle before the besiegers, the gates are no longer defended. And it is on the other side, inside the town, that the fighting continues.

The powerful elephant has been led in front of the principal gate. He knows what they expect of him.......

Taking a firm stand on his legs, placed on the ground like unshakable pillars the magnificent beast attacks with his head the gate of the town. Under his repeated blows, such as those of a huge battering ram, the wooden planks of teak strengthened with iron fittings, moan and collapse. The beast repeats its efforts. Its head moves to and fro, its legs firm on the ground. And these movements finish the resistance of the gate. It cracks, gives way and falls in suddenly. The town is open to the besiegers waiting outside.

Through the large entrance, the soldiers of Honsa rush

in, and the ransack of the town starts.

Not a single house, nor a single hut escapes the soldiers, brave in looting, who scatter over the roads, arms filled with victuals and other booty. There are kitchen utensils, cloths, betel boxes, urns which even the funeral ashes cannot protect.......

And the conquerers gather together young women, who makes every vain endeavour to avoid them. There is no refuge. They must fall prey to the victors.

A messenger brings to the King of Honsa's knowledge the fact that his troops have subdued the town.

Joy is in the King's heart, but it is alloyed by anger against these people who did not allow themselves to be taken by surprise and who compelled him to fight and pay a high price. So divided between contrary feelings, he makes his entry into the conquered town.......

He passes between rows of soldiers lined up on both sides of the principal gate, which had been smashed by the elephants. Behind the soldiers he can see the prisoners tied together, the frightened women squatting on the ground. He stops and casts his eyes over the ruins of the houses and huts which constituted Kanburi......

With a loud voice, he harangues the troops:

"Kanburi is now ours. Kill every man and child. Take the women along with the troops. On to the Capital of Ayodaya!"

But it seems that the answering wails of the women only redouble the anger of the conqueror. Prince Bureng and the Prime Minister who happen to be at the King's side, observe with anxiety his concentrated fury.

Abruptly, the King decides:

"Set fire to the place and burn it to the ground!"

The Prime Minister bows. The command of the King is the supreme law........

Fire! Fire! The King commands fire to be set the town......

One would think that the troops are already waiting for this signal. Men appear from all sides, torches in their hands. They run from house to house. The roofs covered with attap form combustible food for the blaze. The houses are close to each other; the fire jumps from one house to another in no time.

The bamboo with which the houses are built is easy prey. Dried up by days without rain, it crackles and soon the houses are nothing more than a blazing mass.

"Fire! Fire!" shout Honsa's soldiers.

And all the town quickly becomes a burning hell......

It is with this sight that the King of Honsa, with an unpleasant laugh, satisfies his lust for revenge and retires out of the town to join his camp.

CHAPTER XI

NEWS IS BROUGHT TO AYODAYA

King Chakra's Lord Chamberlain dwells in a house situated in the interior of the royal precinct and embellished with spacious verandahs where one rejoices in the breath of the fresh morning air which blows from the river, from the sea that is far away.

He likes to entertain his friends, the nobility of the Kingdom, the Ministers of the Monarch.

Today, they are again together, chewing betel nuts or scrunching fruits, squatting according to custom on a carpet which the Lord Chamberlain had bought at a high price from an itinerant Chinese merchant, who came from the North and was pushing boldly, seeking business, towards the great islands situated in the South, according to the tales of travellers. But those travellers were a curious lot, eager to learn but often inclined to lie when they related stories that none could verfy.

The talk runs on the famous elephant hunt undertaken recently by King Chakra.

It was a great event, which will not easily be forgotten. It is well to repeat the tale again and always in detail in order not to forget it. Memories of the hunt will be transmitted to future generations.

"And so," says the Lord Chamberlain, "the hunt was a

great success, was it? I am glad. For His Majesty can now give his attention to some of the pressing affairs of State......."

He looks at his friend, the War Minister.

"This question of his marriage," he continues, "has got to be settled."

And he adds, with a sigh:

"I cannot understand why a man should go into the jungle looking for excitement when he can find all that he wants by getting married......."

"Yes! Yes!" approves the War Minister with his tongue in his cheek, if this expression can be used where War Ministers are concerned.

"You saw," says the Lord Chamberlain, "the girls I brought for him. Why, even my daughter......."

And he looks complacently at Renoo who raises her eyes only to lower them again with a slightly confused countenance.

"Oh! Well!" continues the fond father. "She made no impression upon him. I cannot understand it."

"You do not try to understand, Father," syas Renoo raising her head and looking at him with her somewhat mocking eyes. "How can you expect His Majesty to be bothered with wives when the country is in danger?"

"Danger, child? Huh! Who is going to attack us? You have been troubling your little head to much with the King's words! Nonsense!"

"I do not know," says Renoo desperately. "But elephants are such lovely creatures and so useful too. I like them!"

"Nonsense, child! Nonsense!" interrupts the father.

And, with a laugh, to the War Minister:

"She does not know what she is talking about."

Then turning to Renoo:

"You had better sing for us, my dear."

And to the Minister:

"Because she can sing, you know. Have you heard her? Sing Renoo, sing one of our old songs for His Excellency the Minister!"

Renoo sighs. She has not ceased thinking of King Chakra since that day; of that Sovereign, a little strange, who does not appreciate dancing and who appears to possess some highly peculiar ideas about the traditional harem.

But she must sing.......

Renoo leans against one of the pillars which support the roof of the house and smiles to all those nobles whom she knows well, who have known her from childhood, even this War Minister who stares at her while curling his moustache and who obviously does not share the prejudice of the King.......

Renoo sings:

Wasna pang kõn t´i yòn sǫ̃ng
Hài rao khong dài rap mai klap hai
Thà tam di di sõng suk mâi wai
Thà tam rài rài sǫ̃ng trong tam do-em
Mà-en pang kon tua khà dài tâm di
Cong sǫ̃ng sri swat p´ip´ at serm
Sõng khwam rak t´i tàng wai ta=e do-em
Hài pun p´o=em samret dang čǎǐ pong.

Past deeds bring their retribution and to each his own desert.

Lasting bliss is the fruit of virtue and naught but ill results from wickedness.

Had I in former lives performed worthy deeds,

Now, if ever, may these further my happiness and aid my love to attain its coveted end.

The music of the vibrating instruments accompanies, with a rhythm slightly doleful, the melancholy song of Renoo.......It dies away with the song, whilst the Lord Chamberlain still keeps his eyes closed, as he always does, in ecstasy, when he hears his daughter sing.

Because he loves his daughter, this Lord Chamberlain. He thinks that nothing in the world is so marvellous as his daughter. If the King decides to follow the old custom, what privileged place could she not obtain among the three hundred and sixty five wives selected?

The gallop of a horse is heard outside the house; the noise makes him re-open his eyes abruptly......

"Beautiful, my dear, beautiful!........."

And turning round to the Minister:

"Was not it?"

"Yes! Yes! very, very beautiful," replies complacently the War Minister, whose eyes are still upon the singer.

But, outside, there is a murmur of voices which reaches them.

One man speaks in a jerky tone.

"It is very urgent. I have to see him......"

The Lord Chamberlain stares and his hesitating eyes search the anxious eyes of the Minister.

They have not to wait for long.

A man, guided by a soldier, in a hurry, has just made his way into room. His clothes are in disorder and covered with dust. Perspiration pours from his face. He is out of breath.

"What is it? What is it?" says the Lord Chamberlain.

"Sir!" says the messenger. "I come from Kanburi. I have been able to escape from the town."

"Escaped?" echoes the Minister.

"Yes! The Honsas attacked us."

The company starts suddenly.

"They have captured Kanburi!" continues the man.

"That is impossible!" says the Lord Chamberlain getting up. It must be reported to the King at once.....

He calls a servant:

"Quick, my clothes......And you," says he to the messenger, "tell me all about it while I am changing"

*   *   *   *   *   *

In hurrying to the royal palace, the War Minister and the Lord Chamberlain exchange words full of dread.

"I am afraid," says the Minister. "I am afraid that we have not taken seriously enough the grave danger which the King did warn us of.........Have we really fulfilled our duty?"

"We are good men and true," protests the Lord Chamberlain. "We are not bad citizens, nor unruly subjects of His Majesty"

"Certainly not," replies the Minister. "No! But that is not enough. We should not have taken deceit for friendship, nor neglected disguised threats because we prefer not to face facts. The awakening is hard......"

"Perhaps," says the Lord Chamberlain. "But have we not the will to victory and, if necessary, to give our lives for it? We shall not betray our people by an abject submission. We prefer any sacrifice to the stigma of a dishonourable peace and we shall refuse to live as slaves tolerated by the King of Honsa. Let us approach our Sovereign with unruffled counterances."

CHAPTER XII
KING CHAKRA THE WARRIOR

King Chakra is finishing his midday meal.

The table at which he is seated is placed on the well ventilated verandah and on the walls hang the finest tapestries made by the craftsmen of Ayodaya.

The King has in front of him some trays filled with numerous fruits.

Looking at the fruits, he counts them absent-mindedly, these fruits with their variegated colours: the guavas, the pulp of the jackfruit extracted from its rough skin, the mangoes still obtainable at the end of the season, the round mangosteens, some red slices of juicy papayas, some sapodillas and also an early durian the smooth and tasty morsels of which rise in an appetising pyramid.

The country of Ayodaya, thinks the King, is blessed by the gods since it gives us such exquisite produce.......

"No bananas today?"

The attendant bows:

"We have no bananas today, Sire. But there are some pomelos...." He holds out the tray to the Sovereign.

"They are better than bananas or grape-fruit," he affirms.

"Fine! Fine!" says the King, taking a pomelo.

He has just started to cut open one of the fruits and to extract the white and juicy pulp packed together when there is a knock at the door of the hall.

King Chakra looks surprised. It is not the time for an audience. Who should come and intrude upon these few rare moments when a King may enjoy a little privacy?

But the knock is louder, and, at a sign from the King, the attendant proceeds to open the door.

He steps backwards at once.

"Their Excellencies the War Minister and the Lord Chamberlain, Sire!"

The King nods:

"Show them in."

Through the wide entrance the two high dignitaries show themselves; the door is closed behind them.

The glance of the King invites them to speak.

The two nobles perform the ritual genuflexion, an action no one ever forgets even in grave circumstances.

Then, hastily, the War Minister explains, his voice unsteady:

"Sire, the King of Honsa has captured Kanburi."

The Lord Chamberlain cuts in............

"He has taken the women prisoner, killed all the men and children, and burned every house in the town."

King Chakra feels his face hot with blood; his countenance expresses a lowering storm not yet broken.

"The King of Honsa has attacked us without a formal declaration of war?" he exclaims. "This is against international custom!"

Now he moves up and down the hall, raising his arms in anger. He goes out on to the balcony, comes back, returns there again, then finally leans against the high balustrade.

"But what can we expect," he continues pursing his lips, "from one whose word cannot be trusted?"

He raises his arm, calling the attention of his Ministers, and speaks to them in a solemn manner.

"Do you remember the episode of Saributta and the two devils?[1]

It happened when the blessed Buddha inhabited the bamboo forest at Racagaha.

There were two monks, Saributta and his friend Maha-Moggallana, who resided in a neighbouring monastery.

One night, when the moon was shining in a perfedtly clear sky, the venerable Saributta came to sit out of doors in order to taste the freshness of the air; and, deep in serious thought, he did not take long to fall into an ecstasy.

Now it came to pass that two devils, who were proceeding elsewhere intent upon evil, did perceive the venerable Saributta, so calm and so far removed from the perishable things of this world.

"Comrade," said the first one, "would it not be a good joke to strike a heavy blow on the shaven head of this **phikkhu**?"

"Comrade," replied the second, "do not attack this **phikkhu,** he is a most holy monk, possessed of supernatural power."

But the first devil insisted upon his idea and thrice repeated his proposition.

Then, ignoring the advice of his comrade, he struck a blow on the head of the venerable Saributta.

It was a heavy blow, indeed, a blow capable of knocking down an elephant of seven cubits in height or to crack a mountain. But thereupon the evil-doer set up a howl: "I am burning! I am burning!" and fell into the hell whence he came.

---

(1) *Udana, IV, 4.*

Maha-Moggallana, the other venerable monk had not failed to perceive that Saributta had been struck on the head by a devil.

He went in haste to enquire after him:

"O my brother, do you find yourself well? Do you feel well? Did not something untoward happen to you?"

"I feel very well, brother Moggallana. I am very well; but I have just a little headache."

"How wonderful, brother Saributta!" exclaimed the other **phikkhu.** "How marvellous are the power and the strength of the venerable Saributta."

"But why all this concern?" asked this latter, surprised.

"It is that a devil has struck you a fromidable blow, a blow to knock out an elephant seven cubits high or to crack a mountain. And, in the meanwhile, the venerable Saributta has nothing more to say then that he feels quite well, except that he has a little headache!"

Now, the Blessed One, whose divinely keen ear surpassed those of men, heard this conversation and uttered these unforgettable words:

"The man whose spirit, as a rock,

"Remains impassible and cannot be perturbed;

"Whom no pleasure can excite,

"Whom no provocation can wrath,

"He who has well trained his spirit,

"What misfortune can befall him?"

"Now then! Ayodaya must remain as unshakble as the venerable Saributta, when the devils who inhabit the other side of the hills come to attack her without reason. And, as the venerable Saributta, she will throw them into hell by reason of her virtues......"

King Chakra concludes and turns to the War Minister:

"Get your army ready. We will go out to meet him."

"It shall be done, Sire!" says the Minister, moving off hastily.

King Chakra leans on the balcony, his brows knit, gazing vacantly at the high roofs of the royal buildings, the colonnades of the temples, these ancient glories of Ayodaya which stretch in front of him and are in danger of the fury of the conqueror.

The Lord Chamberlain shakes his head......

He takes a step to follow the War Minister. He takes two more to draw nearer the King. He hesitates. Then he decides. Time must not be lost, the moments are precious.

Bowing ceremoniously, he speaks to the Monarch.

"May it please Your Majesty......"

King Chakra turns and looks at him inquiringly.

"Your Majesty," he proceeds timidly, "will not forget to observe the custom before going to war?"

"Do not talk about the question of wives again," says Chakra with anger. "While I am away, you stay in the Capital and see to the welfare of the people."

CHAPTE XIII
IN BATTLE ARRAY

Here is the army of Ayodaya on its war-footing: infantry, cavalry and numerous elephants, the pride and the wealth of the nation, dressed for battle and moving impatiently.

On his fighting elephant, the War Minister leads the host.

They are here, all these troops prepared for merciless battle, standing as if at a ceremonial inspection. And, when King Chakra appears on his elephant, it is the usual sound of conches and trumpets which welcome him; the men salute.

The royal elephant passes slowly in front of the troops.

Chakra reviews proudly the elephants dressed for war, and well trained for battle. He calculates the number of his horsemen, on the backs of their small ponies, the breed of the country, swift and sure on their legs, accustomed to difficult runs through ricefields rough and full of obstacles. He contemplates with satisfaction the ranks of infantrymen, well disciplined, well formed, well armed. Well then! He had often carried out similar inspection in peace time. But now there are other preoccupations..........

The royal elephant has stopped towards the middle of the front row of the troops, whom the King now addresses:

"My beloved people! As you know by now our country has been attacked by Hon̄sa. Kanburi has fallen, and the enemy is heading straight for our Capital. We will not wait for him, but will go out to meet him......"

There is a hum of approbation.

"The King of Honsa," continues Chakra, "is fighting for his personal ambition, but he is making his people pay for it with their lives......"

Chakra looks round at his men:

"We are fighting against aggression. Remember! We fight not against the people of Honsa, but against their Ruler......"

"I shall expect," ends the King, "each of you to do your duty for your King and country."

"Forward! Forward!" is shouted from all sides.

And, without delay, as they have already received instructions, the officers shout out brief orders. The soldiers prepare to march in columns of route. The whole army moves off and leaves the parade-ground to march across the country.

On the outskirts of the Capital, the daily routine of life has not yet been disturbed by the threat of war. The paddy-fields are being worked by the primitive ploughs drawn by buffaloes, strong on their legs and possessed of enormous heads with crumpled horns.

One sees other farmers making themselves busy in flooding the fields, draining the water from the canal nearby and helping to distribute it along the channels which cross the plain.

They all stop to look at the army which advances and, when they perceive the King at its head, they make much effort, according to custom and out of respect for the Royal Majesty, to hide themselves, to disappear, to make themselves as inconspicuous as possible.

It is a happy picture of agricultural life, lived by a country which looks forward only to peace and prosperity. Why, thinks King Chakra in contemplating the scene, why, is it necessary that those birds of prey should come and threaten with their violence these innocent and hard-working beings? And anger blazes in his indignant heart.

CHAPTER XIV

ON THE EVE OF BATTLE

"**O**ver there camps Honsa's army!" says King Chakra, gazing at the horizon from the back of his elephant.

He is far away from Ayodaya now.

Here, it is open-country, thinly populated. The bushes extend as far as the eye can reach, but one can perceive groups of men on the far horizon.

For over there the King of Honsa has ordered his troops to make camp. He has himself just joined them, and stopping near the fence, is inspecting the military arrangements and the prisoner brought from Kanburi.

Prince Bureng guides him.

"Here is the camp prepared for you, Sire! Everything is ready: food, wine and women. They are at your pleasure."

Honsa fastens his leather belt, his eyes distended by lust in surveying the female prisoners massed in a corner.

"Good!..........Very good!.........."

And with steps which the first fatigue of the war make heavy, he goes towards the hut which has been arranged for his use.

Yes, all is ready in this hut. The servants know the tastes of the master. To be more sure of satisfying them, here is the first steward who himself tastes the liquor prefered by the Monarch (and, after, all, by himself)..........

The King arrives and takes his place on the divan whilst the high officers who accompany him settle themselves here and there.

"Sire," says the steward, "this wine is made from the very best rice of Ayodaya."

"Huh! Huh!" says Honsa..........

And he tastes it as an enlightened connoisseur.

"Quite good! Quite good! Give me some more. Give me some more."

Glasses succeed one another, but hardly quick enough to satisfy the impatience of the King.

"Bring in the women-prisoners!" he shouts to the Prime Minister."

The order is given..........

*   *   *   *   *   *

All round the royal hut are the troops of Honsa. They are resting after the hard fighting at Kanburi and cooking rice and fish for the evening meal.

Good-tempered and relieved of his state robes, the Prime Minister is among them. His is a happy soul. The King is busy, so one can enjoy quietly the sweetness of the hour.

Victorious soldiers like music and dance thinks the Prime Minister of the King of Honsa.

And, clapping his hands, he orders that dances accompanied by the sound of tambourins be started.

Amateur-musicians are numerous. Soon, one by one, they are up and dancing round the fire, lit to divert both the mosquitoes and the evil spirits.

The Prime Minister finishes his meal. This war gives him, indeed, a formidable appetite. Here is chicken a la sauce......He has never felt himself in such good form. Here is curry with perfumed herbs and spices. All is going well, and they will, no doubt, reach Ayodaya in a few days. A little bit of that smoked fish which comes from the sea far away......

The Prime Minister sighs with satisfaction.

Ah! The men dance and the air rings with the tambourins.......This reminds him of his childhood, during which he was not yet overwhelmed with the worries of power and the fear of bringing about a change in the King of Honsa's humour.

Dancing favours digestion, thinks the Prime Minister. Why not? He gets up, he joins the drummers, he takes a vague step.......The crowd of soldiers applaude. Ah! He is a good fellow, and not haughty, the Prime Minister.

He finishes the night out of doors, snoring in spite of the mosquitoes to which his tanned skin in no prey, and is awakened by a too greedy guard, who attempting to steal a bit of the ministerial curry makes the mistake of allowing the cover of the pot to fall with a crash.

CHAPTER XV

HERE COMES THE ARMY OF AYODAYA !

The sun rises on the rice-field and on the jungles of the country of the White Elephant.

It dissipates the last fumes which crawl close to the ground during the damp of the night.

The army of King Chakra has answered the reveille. It is already on the march, before the powerful heat appears in the middle of the day.

The land on which they have to march is welltimbered. Sometimes also, it changes into a real forest, and trees rise in high columns from among the bushes.

The elephants pass first: they go straight ahead, suppressing, with their trunks or foreheads any obstacles which may bar their path. Thus is the way made clear for the infantry and cavalry.

Such movements have not been unnoticed. Hidden on trees, the scouts of Honsa's army are quick-witted when they see that enemy detachments are advancing. They catch their horses hidden in the bushes, and gallop towards the royal camp to warn their chiefs.

"Hi! Hi! Here comes the army of Ayodaya!"

And whilst this army treads its way rapidly through the forest and the jungle, the camp of the King of Honsa is in a bustle.

But nothing reaches the ears of the Monarch.......

CHAPTER XVI
THE BATTLE IS JOINED

Prince Bureng - may disgust be ejected from his heart - has joined his troop of war elephants and taken the place befitting his rank and duty.

He had just returned from a most unpleasant audience with his King. On receiving the scouts' report he had straightaway gone to his royal uncle to inform him of this unexpected turn of events, pausing only to give orders for the alarm and the general muster to be sounded. Arriving at the hut he had hastened past the guards into the royal presence, only to find that the King was already up - but not in response to the call to arms that was then resounding throughout the camp. It was other arms that the King of Honsa was interested in - the arms of two of the fairest of the women prisoners whom he had retained the night before. Seated on his bed he held each by the arm and pulled first one and then the other towards him as each shrank back against his advances.

Overcoming his first repugnance at the sight, Bureng had blurted out the bad news. "Bad?" had reechoed the King of Honsa, unheeding, "Bad? Who says she's bad?" Bureng had need of all his self-control to keep his voice calm as he reiterated the news and asked for orders for the fight. The last word caught the ears of the King. "Fight! That's it, fight!" he had drunkenly affirmed, drawing one of the girls towards him,

"I'll fight with this one!" Bureng had left at that, to take command himself of the army. So this was the kind of man whose mere word was even now sending thousands of men to their death. But what could a subject, especially a soldier do, except to obey?

So Bureng, now seated on his war-elephant, stands up, and with a sweep of the arm gives the word of command:

"Forward!"

The detachments of the army group themselves together and move. They spread now into the plain and the two opposing armies will shortly come face to face.

The soldiers armed with rifles give the signal for the fight, with their long range weapons which overcome distance.

On both sides, the riflemen exchange fire. Some men fall. A rifle bursts and kills its owner.

But these preliminaries make the warriors impatient.

"At them," shout the soldiers of Ayodaya running through the thickets which sheltered them.

"Charge! Charge!" replies Prince Bureng urging on his men with voice and gesture.

And a hand to hand fight starts, pitiless, bloody, terrible, and magnificent. The brave meet the brave. Their hearts lose no strength. Their duty is to kill, and also to be killed, if such is necessary.....

This is war..........

Why should elephants be less pugnacious than men? Here they are on both sides......They roar with anger....... blow the dust from the ground.......They clash.......They push each other back.......Misfortune to the one which loses its balance and falls: it disappears in the deadly tide which breaks on it.

In the forest, the cavalry of Chakra waits impatiently for the order which sounds at last:

"Cavalry! Mount!"

Their eagerness has to be controlled.

"Wait! Wait!" yells an aide-de-camp. "His Majesty's commands are that you are to wait here till the enemy's cavalry appears. Then, you are to attack them on the flank."

The horsemen grunt but have to obey.

They realise that, over there, the two hostile infantries are engaged in the fight, charging one against the other, backed by the elephants.......

The cavalry of Honsa too is waiting under shelter. But they do not display any eagerness. The soldiers are sleeping on the grass and smoking quietly. They even show bad temper when an aide-de-camp comes towards them and turning to the officer in command exclaims:

"Sir! Prince Bureng orders the cavalry to attack at once."

The officer shakes his head:

"We do not take orders from Prince Bureng," he says, "where is our King?"

The aide-de-camp replies with impatience:

"Prince Bureng has taken command in the name of the King. You will have to obey orders, otherwise it is mutiny."

But the officer persists:

"The cavalry will not move unless the King commands us to. Tell Prince Bureng that."

"And," says a cavalryman of Honsa, "I shall not move until I have finished my smoke......!"

Over there, the battle has taken a new phase. King Chakra stirs up the fight by his presence, while the absence of Honsa, on the contrary, discourages his troops.

Assaulted in front by hot-headed soldiers, hustled on its flanks by the war elephants, the infantry of Honsa hesitates, recoils, falls back. Prince Bureng exhorts them, but nobody listens to him.   Where is the King, at the time when breaks that storm for which he craved?   The men begin to hasten their retreat.   Bureng realises that all is lost and rushes on his horse towards the supporting line.

CHAPTER XVII

CEASE FIRE !

King Chakra's heart is full of pride.

He has seen the defeat of the invader, the murderers of his well beloved subjects.

But some soldiers mounted on their elephants have just come near him.

They point out an enemy elephant.

"That looks like the King of Honsa over there, Sire!"

The blood of Chakra boils in his veins. He feels suddenly a salutary heat rising to his forehead like an encouragement given by the gods.

He orders his elephant to be taken towards the place designated and enjoins the whole army to follow him.

Here before his eyes stands the warlike mount of the devastating King, and they will at last be face to face, man to man.

King Chakra holds up his hand and his troops halt.

"So it is. Stay where you are. I am going to challenge him to fight man to man. Do not harm any more of his men. Take them prisoners if you will. Remember! We have not come to fight the people of Honsa, but only their Leader."

The army is waiting anxiously.

No one takes any notice of the cavalry which, over there, hidden in the wood, chafes under restraint, angry not to be allowed to take its part in the fight....

"Come on, men!" shouts the officer last. "We cannot wait about here all day. Come on!"

"Go on! Go on!" repeat the men already pushing forward their mounts.

But who arrives over there, galloping at full speed? An aide-de-camp of King Chakra. He jumps in front of the horsemen and signals them to stop:

"Wait! Wait! The enemy has been routed and the King has ordered the "Cease fire!" He is going to fight the King of Honsa in single combat."

The news spread among the horsemen who hesitate between the joy caused by this good news and the irritation of having taken no part in the vicotry.

Now, the whole army of Ayodaya is informed. They shiver with impatience, expecting the announced combat, the duel between the two Kings. The officers and the soldiers exchange their views and extol the courage and the virtue of Chakra, the Monarch who prefers to risk his own life rather than that of his subjects.

CHAPTER XVIII
KINGS IN SINGLE COMBAT

On his war elephant, King Chakra proceeds at a slow trot towards the camps where the King of Honsa has seen his panic-stricken troops running back.

The news spreads among the warriors who cease to move, awaiting an extraordinary event.

King Chakra arrives before the hostile camp and waits.

But, in the meantime, the aides-de-camp of Honsa have managed to surround his elephant. There are four or five of them. King Chakra will be caught he will be killed.

The King raises himself up on his seat and speaking in a loud voice:

"Stay! Listen, Soldiers of Honsa! I am in your hands and you can kill me if you will. But though I may perish, my Kingdom of Ayodaya will still live on. That, you will never be able to destroy. You do not need the sound of my victorious troops to remind you of that. But my quarrel is not with you. I am here to seek your King. For he alone is responsible for all this bloodshed between us. Let him come forth and fight me man to man!"

The aides-de-camp hesitate. Is it a trap which has been laid for them? Who is this King who, instead of leaving his troops to fight, comes alone, by himself to challenge their Lord and Master......

They hesitate and look at each other.

But the voice of Honsa now makes itself heard.

"Come on!" he exclaims. "I will fight him. I will kill him. Soldiers! Leave him to me. I will kill him myself. Let him through!"

The aides-de-camp move aside and the elephant of King Chakra, resuming its rhythmical march, advances towards that of Honsa, followed at a distance by the aides-de-camp always ready to intervene.

King Chakra has nothing for them but a smile of contempt.

And in a mocking tone to the King of Honsa:

"Brother!" he says. "What are you waiting for? A scion of a royal stock you are, and a scion of a kingly race am I. It behoves us to fight upon our elephants so that all these men may see and take delight therein...."

He glances at the opposing army rooted to the spot:

"Let us fight this out man to man," he continues. "Let us not sacrifice the lives of our soldiers. It is for us two, men and descendants of Kings, to fight in single combat. For, in future, no King will there be to engage in a similar duel."

And, composing his voice, which trembles with anger:

"For after all it is for your own personal ambition that you have forced this war on us and not for the one single white elephant. It is not just to risk the life of our men."

The King of Honsa leans forward on the neck of his enormous beast.

"Brother!" he replies in a harsh voice. "I think you are right. A King should fight a King and not sacrifice the lives of his people. I accept your challenge."

The die is cast.

The two magnificent beasts are rushing towards each

other. They roar with fury. One would think that they understand the part they have to play and know that they each carry a powerful Sovereign at the moment when the issue of the war is to be decided.

The two monarchs have been trained since childhood for these single combats where the sword and the spear take a prominent part. As soon as the elephants heads come together, the duel starts.

Honsa attacks with fury, flourishing his spear, and straightaway Chakra confines himself to parrying the blow with the woodenhandle of his own weapon. He plays for time to allow his antagonist to become exhausted. The air re-echoes with the sound of repeated blows. Then the two men give up the spear which is too cumbersome, and with the glaive - the royal bent glaives - they continue their fight. Their glaives are flashing.

"For you!" says Honsa, who strikes with all his power a blow which he believes adequate to smash the head of his opponent.

But the trained elephant of Chakra turns aside and the heavy stroke misses its mark.

It is Chakra now who leans forward, with an arm raised, above Honsa who is busy keeping his balance. The arm is lowered once, twice. The King of Honsa staggers, tries to catch hold of the neck of his beast, then, his strength exhausted, falls from the large shoulder and crashes to the ground.

CHAPTER XIX
CHAKRA'S FORBEARANCE

The soldiers of Ayodaya, mounted on their elephants, see the defeat of the King of Honsa. They make exulting cries. They rush forward like an avalanche, pushing before them the troops of Honsa who step back in disorder.

Fighting will be resumed, a massacre will surely take place......

But King Chakra has raised himself on his elephant, flourishing his warflag, and a gesture from him stops his troops.

"Stop! Stop!" he cries. "Do not harm them. They have no quarrel with us. We fought against the King of Honsa, and now the King of Honsa is no more......."

His finger points at the wounded monarch who is dying at the feet of his restless elephant, surrounded by his aides-de-camp.

"Bring the prisoners," continues Chakra.

Hastily, the enemy officers and soldiers are gathered together in front of the elephant of the Monarch of Ayodaya. In the first row are Prince Bureng and the Prime Minister. Their heads are bowed, because they have never approved of the campaign imposed on them by the vanity of their King, and which has now been lost through his defeat. They do not even regret his death; he has well deserved it. But what will happen to them, now that they are in the power of the enemy?

Chakra looks at all these men, still moved by anxiety for their personal safety. Their fate lies in his hands. But he thinks of the Stanza which he likes so much:

"Not hatred for hatred......"[1]

Then he takes his decision:

"Listen all," he exclaims, "O Chiefs and Soldiers of Honsa. You know of the friendship that once bound me to the King of Honsa. Nevertheless insults did he heap upon me. I am a man like him and yet he took me for a slave. This was the real reason of my anger and this is why I wished to have this duel with him. Now am I satisfied, seeing that he has perished by my own hands. I shall return to Ayodaya, my City."

King Chakra looks round at the prisoners with compassion in his eyes.

"Soldiers of Honsa! You have been misled into a war with us, we who always wished to live in peace with you. You now stand defeated before us, but we will not wreak vengence on you for all the harm you have done us.........Return all to your homes."

The people of Honsa lift up their head. Hope now shines on their countenance.

"Let this be a lesson to you," continues Chakra, "a lesson to all of us. Never allow yourselves to be driven like dumb cattle again......."

The Monarch raises his hand:

"Tell your children and your children's children of this day, when King fought King in single combat to settle their differences, so that future generations may know and compel

---

(1) From *Tharmapada, Khuddaya, Nikaya* or *Buddhistic Stanza of the Khunddaka-Nikaya Section.*

their leaders to do likewise, if fight they must. In that way alone can the peoples of our world be spared useless wars and unnecessary sufferings."

King Chakra turns then towards his own troops:

"You have, today, seen your comrades and your beloved ones slain before your very eyes......."

A tremor goes through the ranks.

"Many of you will bear scars of today's fight for the rest of your lives......."

Stretching out his arms in a single gesture of reconciliation, Chakra concludes:

"Let not these scars eat into your hearts. Bear no malice towards one another for what has taken place today........Our dead demand this of us......."

Then ends the royal speech:

"Soldiers of Honsa! Take up your arms and return to your homes, and may peace be with you."

Prince Bureng bows silently, and, turning towards his troops, he commands them to recover the weapons which they had piled up in front of the royal elephant.

King Chakra lifts his spear:

"Soldiers of Ayodaya! Do honour to your brothers of Honsa."

"Chayo! Chayo! Chayo!" thrice shout victors.

Prince Bureng replies, raising his sowrd:

"Soldiers of Honsa! Salute Chakra, King of the White Elephant, noble in name and in nature as noble. Long live the King of the White Elephant!"

"Hurrah! Hurrah! Hurrah!" shout the vanquished.

Chakra happily contemplates this scene of reconciliation, the fruit of his own desire.

"Henceforth," he says turning towards Prince Bureng,

"let there be mutual understanding and good-will between us, and may Peace, once more, reign over us and all our sister nations of the world for evermore. And by the protecting grace of the Triple Gems and the sacred Powers in the Universe may such Peace be everlasting. Farewell."

"Farewell, Sire," replies Prince Bureng.

The whole army of Honsa moves. They make their way back. The elephants first, then the infantry and the cavalry amongst whom many wounded may be seen, wearing bandages or hobbling along without being able to keep step.

On the horizon, the sun sets on the open-country of Ayodaya; and the satisfied soldiers of Chakra, cheerfully moving in their turn towards the Capital, exulting in the joy of victory and happy in the possession of a wise, magnanimous and merciful Sovereign.

CHAPTER XX
AYODAYA TRIUMPHANT

The victorious troops have cleared their country of the enemy.

Here they are, returning to Ayodaya, led by King Chakra who smiles while passing, carried on his palanquin through the crowded rows of the people, flocking up to pay him respect.

Every one is happy to get back to his home and the King rejoices at the thought of seeing that palace which he left with an anxious heart, uncertain as to the future of his beloved people.

All is finished, happily. Life will resume its peaceful development, and the King will be able to keep himselrf busy with the progressive reform by which he desired to assure the welfare of the Kingdom.

The procession stops in front of the royal terrace where there are steps by which the King, coming down from his palanquin, returns into his palace. Here he recognises, with much happiness, the loyal faces of his Ministers and faithful servants.

They are all here, happy and gay, and the Lord Chamberlain is not the last to present his homage.

Victory, victory of the armies of Ayodaya, that is also a tradition, to be maintained by future generations: is not this moment, at last, a most auspicious one?

The Lord Chamberlain has no doubt of it and it is with a smile that he says to the King:

"The war is now ended! What about the custom, Sire?"

A wrinkle of the eyebrows of the Monarch answers him:

"Your three hundred and sixty-five wives, I suppose?"

The Lord chamberlain lifts up his hands, imploring:

"Honsa's record was three hundred and sixty six, Your Majesty! For the honour of our country, you will now have to take three hundred and sixty six.......I have brought some very beautiful girls for Your Majesty's selection......."

He indicates the motionless and perplexed group which tries to catch, but is also frightened at, the gaze of the King.

He looks rather impatient, that King, and he undoubtedly prefers other business which has for him much more interest.

But the Lord Chamberlain by no means perceives it and, quite merry, bends ingratiatingly towards his Sovereign :

"If you do not wish to choose all the three hundred and sixty five wives now, you can choose one first......."

His fatherly pride takes him further.

"My daughter is here, too......"

Here is, in fact, the beautiful Renoo, dressed on this day of glory in the most beautiful cloths manufactured by the craftsmen of Ayodaya; she has her hair crowned with flowers suitable for the occasion and her smile greets the King as the dawn that warms and illuminates the early morning sky.

Renoo.......After all, he has not forgotten her, this attractive Renoo with her intelligent and deep eyes, the prettiest girl, no doubt in the Kingdom of Ayodaya.

She is here, in front of him, making the ritual salute and thrilling with an unutterable emotion.

Chakra smiles a little, ponders for one moment, and,

turning toward the Lord Chamberlain :

"To save us from any more of your importunities, we will give in.......and choose as our first wife.......your daughter."

The Lord Chamberlain stands erect, tremulous with agitation.

"But," continues the King, "we wish to raise from now on our first wife to the position of an "Honorary Queen", without any pension or palace."

He considers one moment :

"As for the other three hundred and sixty five wives, I shall choose them myself, later."

Then, turning round, Chakra moves towards the steps of the palace, leaving his Lord Chamberlain astounded.

The latter can hardly believe his own ears. But he is not at the end of his worries. Now his daughter herself, his dear Renoo - Honorary Queen - puts the blame on him.

"It's just like you, father. Did I not tell you that you did not understand His Majesty. You have spoilt everything!"

"Nonsense, child! Nonsense!" splutters the unfortunate father.

But Renoo has already left him.

King Chakra ascends slowly the steps which lead to his rooms. Perhaps he has already forgotten this incident, the incident of the Honorary Queen.......Perhaps!

But behind him, Renoo mounts the stairs, in her turn, and bows at his feet.

"May it please Your Majesty, though I am just an Honorary Queen, may I be permitted to say that the upkeep of three hundred and sixty five wives would be better employed to increase the welfare of the people and the prosperity of the country."

Chakra's interest is aroused on hearing these words. He looks with more interest at this young girl whose graceful charms he had not noticed up to now.

He smiles to her, encouragingly.

"Even though the war is over," continues Renoo, "We still have need of elephants, not only for the Army, but for work in our forests......."

And she adds naively :

"Besides, elephants are such lovely creatures. I like them........."

This time, King Chakra laughs frankly.

"Your Majesty," continues Renoo emboldened, "would do better to spend your money on the upkeep of elephants. Do not pay any attention to father."

King Chakra begins to think that he has found a woman according to his heart.

He calls again the Lord Chamberlain :

"Why! my dear Lord Chamberlain, you have a very intelligent daughter........."

The face of the gentleman blossoms out into a smile.

"Yes!" continues the King. "A very wise daughter, wiser than her father......."

The smile ends in a grimace.

The King has, however, taken the arm of Renoo and says to her :

"My dear, it shall be as you say, but you will have to help me. You seem to be the only one who understands me. The more I look at you the more I like you. Will you be my Queen, my *real* Queen?"

There is no more question of an Honorary Queen!

Renoo flushes with pleasure. She makes the ritual genuflexion.

"Your Majesty is very gracious!"

She kisses the hand of the Monarch as a token of obedience, and adds :

"If you want to put an end to the custom once for all, you can......"

She whispers some words in a low voice.

"Oh!" says the King smiling with pleasure and nodding. He calls :

"My Lord Chamberlain?"

"Sire!" replies the latter, approaching with eagerness.

The King meditates one moment, then :

"Is there a custom......that a King may confer any of his royal prerogatives upon anybody that he chooses?"

The Lord Chamberlain opens his eyes wide and scratching the back of his head :

"There is, Your Majesty," he replies at last.

"Fine! Fine!" says Chakra.

And raising his voice so that all may hear :

"In that case, we formally renounce henceforth our prerogative of having three hundred and sixty five wives for ourselves and for our heirs and successors forevermore......"

An interval.

"And it is our pleasure that this prerogative be henceforth conferred upon our Lord Chamberlain."

The latter moves one step backward.

"But..........er..........Your Majesty, is not that too many?"

"No! Not too many, my dear Lord Chamberlain," replies the King. "We must not be beaten by Honsa. At least, we have to equal his record. We command you strictly to observe this custom for us."

And, turning towards the new Queen :

"As for us, let us go and find ourselves three hundred and sixty five more elephants, shall we, dear?"

"Yes! Yes! Your Majesty," says Renoo joyfully.

CHAPTER XXI
PEACE EVERLASTING

Dreams materialize sometimes.....

Whilst the Lord Chamberlain follows, with an affectionate look, King Chakra and his daughter who make their way towards the royal palace, Renoo turns round and stops one moment.

"Good-bye, Father........."

Chakra smiles and repeats :

"Good-bye, Father. How are you feeling?"

"Fine, Your Majesty," stammers the Lord Chamberlain. "I am feeling fine!"

"Are you happy, Sire?" asks the coquettish Renoo.

"Terribly happy, my dear," replies Chakra, leading her up the steps.

But realities are not always as perfect as dreams :

"Kine of the White Elephant!" says the Lord Chamberlain, who feels on his shoulders the burden of the wives to come..........

And turning to his friend the War Minister :

"Can you believe it? He loves his country and his elephants more than the idea of having three hundred and sixty six wives!"

"It is," replies the Minister, "because he sees thereby the way to avoid future wars : wise he is, because there is no bliss surpassing Peace - *'n' atthi santiparan sukhan'* "

THE END.

THE KING OF THE WHITE ELEPHANT

Story by

Pridi Banomyong

Directed by

Suhn Vasudhara

Assistant Directors

Luang Sukhum

Chai Suvanadat

Supervised by

Pridi Banomyong

Assistant Supervisor

Prasart Sukhum A.S.C.

Photographed by

Prasart Sukhum A.S.C.

Sound Recorded by

Charn Bunnag

Edited by

Bamrung Naewband

Musical Director

Phra Chen Duriyanga

THE KING OF THE WHITE ELEPHANT

Art Director
M.C. Yachai Chitrabongse

Dialogue
Daeng Guna Tilaka

Master of the elephants
Vongse Saensiribhan

Adviser on ceremonies and costumes
Phya Devadhiraj

Produced at
the Thai Film Studios Bangkok, Thailand

King Chakra :	Renu Kritayakorn
Lord Chamberlain of Ayodaya :	Suvat Nilsen
Ministry of War of Ayodaya :	Luang Srisurang
Renoo Daughter of the :	Pailin Nilsen
Lord Chamberlain	
Governor of Kanburi :	Nit Mahakanok
King of Honsa :	Pradab Rabilvongse
Prince Boreng of Honsa :	Vaivit V. Tipipaks
Prince Minister of Honsa :	Luang Smak
Lord Chamberlain of Honsa :	Prasarn Sripites
Aide - De- Camp to the :	Malai Raktaprachit
Prince Minister of Honsa	

Appendix

International Enquiry:

" Centenary of the Cinema "

Films-Phares

uestionnaire to be copied and to be sent soonest possible to:

International Council for Film, Television and Audiovisual Communica

UNESCO,   1, rue Miollis, 75015 Paris

Fax : 45 67 28 40)

Country : **THAILAND**

Name of person completing the questionaire: **DOME SUKVONG**

Designation of person completing the questionaire: **ARCHIVIST**

Address and telephone no. of person completing the questionnaire :

Address: **National Film Archive**
4 Chaofa Road
Bangkok 10200   THAILAND

Telephone no. : **(662) 281-0170 , (662) 240-1145**

Fax : **(662) 280-1145**

In your country, the film regarded a masterpiece of national heritage
is called : **KING OF THE WHITE ELEPHANT**

Produced by : **Dr. Pridi Banomyong**

in (year of production) : **1940**

(p. 100-101) Documents from the Thai government nominating *The King of the White Elephant* by Dr. Pridi Banomyong to be recognized as a "National treasure" to participate in the 100th World Film Festival organized by UNESCO (March 1994).

Format (16 or 35 mm. only) : __16 mm.__

Duration : __100 min.__

A copy of the film is kept at : __National Film Archive__

The master copy is kept at : __Library of Congress__, USA.

Our country has a film library, ~~does not have a film library~~.

(Delete what does not apply)

If your country has a film library, please give address and, if possibel,

name of person in charge : __Mr. Adisak Sekrattana__

(p. 102-105) Posters and programs of the movie from the 100th World Film Festival. *The King of the White Elephant* was one of the fifty films screened at the festival and it was shown on January 17, 1995 at 18:00 hrs.

A l'occasion de la célébration du

Centenaire du cinéma

Federico Mayor
Directeur général de l'Organisation des Nations Unies
pour l'éducation, la science et la culture

Catherine Deneuve
Ambassadeur de bonne volonté de l'Organisation des Nations Unies
pour l'éducation, la science et la culture

Robert Daudelin
Président de la Fédération internationale des archives du film

ont le plaisir de vous inviter
à participer aux activités organisées avec la coopération
des Commissions nationales pour l'UNESCO

au Siège de l'UNESCO
7, place de Fontenoy – Paris 7ᵉ
du 10 au 22 janvier 1995

P R O G R A M M E

Festival de films restaurés ou retrouvés sur le thème de la tolérance

Mardi 10 janvier
Salle I   15 h 00   *Pinocchio* (Italie), Giulio Antamoro, 1911, 40mn
                   Bartek Zwycierzca (Pologne), Edward Puchalski, 1922, 40mn
       18 h 00   *Willy Reilly and his Colleen Bawn* (Irlande), John Macdonagh, 1920, 1h 30mn
       20 h 30   *Vingarna* (Suède), de Mauritz Stiller, 1916, 40mn
                   Körkarlen (Suède), Victor Sjöström, 1920, 1h 15mn

Mercredi 11 janvier
Salle XI   15 h 00   *Wend Kuuni* (Burkina Faso), Gaston Kaboré, 1982, 1h 10mn
       18 h 00   *Dolina miru* (Slovénie), Stiglic France, 1956, 1h 20mn
       20 h 30   *Largo viaje* (Chili), Patricio Kaulen, 1967, 1h 30mn

Jeudi 12 janvier
Salle I   15 h 00   *Danses et coutumes de Macédoine* (Ex-République yougoslave de Macédoine), Yanaki et Milton Manaki, 1907-1911, 10mn
                   Ned med vaabene (Danemark), Holger-Madsen, 1914, 1h 15mn
       18 h 00   *Die Stadt Ohne Juden* (Autriche), Hans Karl Breslauer, 1924, 1h 24mn
       20 h 30   *La vocation d'André Carel* (Suisse), Jean Choux, 1924, 45mn

Vendredi 13 janvier
Salle I   15 h 00   *Almost Arcady* (Chypre), réalisateur inconnu, 1929, 1h
                   Daphnis et Chloé (Grèce), Orestis Laskos, 1931, 1h 8 mn
       18 h 00   *Janosik 21* (Slovaquie), Jaroslav Siakel, 1921, 1h 5mn
       20 h 30   *The sentimental bloke* (Australie), Raymond Longford, 1919, 1h 8mn

Samedi 14 janvier
Salle I   15 h 00   *El terror de la frontera* (Equateur), Luis Martinez Quirola, 1929, 5mn 30s
                   The Arctic Patrol (Canada), Richard S. Finnie, 1929, 50mn
       18 h 00   *Rojo no Reikon* (Japon), Minoru Murata, 1921, 1h 53mn
       20 h 30   Film-surprise présenté par les Archives du Film (Bois d'Arcy)

Lundi 16 janvier
Salle XI   15 h 00   *La fondation de la République démocratique du Laos* (R.D.P. Lao), Somtheu Phetmany, 1975, 30mn
                   Programme de courts métrages du Pérou et de Puerto Rico
                   The Game: good morning (Jordanie)
       18 h 00   *La escalinata* (Venezuela), César Enriquez, 1950, 1h 30mn
       20 h 30   *Déjà s'envole la fleur maigre* (Belgique), Paul Meyer, 1960, 1h 25mn

Mardi 17 janvier
Salle XI   15 h 00   *Shunko* (Argentine), Lautaro Murua, 1960, 1h 16mn
       18 h 00   *The King of the White Elephant* (Thaïlande), Sunh Vasudhara, 1941, 1h 40mn
       20 h 30   *El-Kalaa* (Algérie), Mohamed Chouikh, 1988, 1h 35mn

Mercredi 18 janvier
Salle XI   15 h 00   *Andreï Roublev* (Fédération de Russie), Andreï Tarkovsky, 1966-1967, 3 h 6mn
       18 h 00   *We leave for England* (Norvège), Toralf Sando, 1946, 2h
       20 h 30   *Budapesti tavasz* (Hongrie), Félix Mariassy, 1955

Jeudi 19 janvier
Salle XI   15 h 00   *Aniki Bobó* (Portugal), Manoel de Oliveira, 1942, 1h 10mn
         18 h 00   *O Místo na slunci* (Rép. tchèque), Frantisek Vystrcil, 1959, 5 mn
                    Myslenka hledající svetlo (Rép. tchèque), Karel èt Irena Dodalovi, 1938, 9mn
                    Bilá nemoc (Rép. tchèque), Hugo Haas, 1937, 1h 45mn
         20 h 30   *Kameradschaft* (Allemagne), G.W. Pabst, 1931, 1h 30mn

Vendredi 20 janvier
Salle XI   15 h 00   *Moseka* (Zaïre), Kwami Mambu Zinga, 1971, 27mn
                    La Noire de... (Sénégal), Sembène Ousmane, 1966, 1h 5mn
         18 h 00   *Connaissez-vous vous-même* (Ukraine), Rolan Sergenko, 40mn
                    Le défilé des 500.000 manifestants de la Bastille à la Porte de Vincennes, le 14 juillet 1935 (France), 1935, 10mn
                    Description d'un combat (Israël), Chris Marker, 1961, 58mn
         20 h 30   *Morena clara* (Espagne), Florian Rey, 1935, 1h 52mn

Samedi 21 janvier
Salle XI   15 h 00   *Le couronnement du Roi Pierre 1ᵉʳ de Serbie* (Royaume-Uni/Serbie), Arnold Meier Willson, 1904, 33mn
                    Broken barrier (Nouvelle-Zélande), Roger Mirams et John O'Shea, 1952, 71mn
         18 h 00   *Shejari* (Inde), V. Shantaram 1941, 2h 25mn
         20 h 30   *Muna Moto* (Cameroun), J.P. Dikongue Pipa, 1975, 1h 40mn

Dimanche 22 janvier
Salle I   15 h 00   *Beyrouth ya Beyrouth* (Liban), Maroun Bagdadi, 1974, 1h 50mn
       20 h 00   *A matter of life and death* (Royaume-Uni), Michael Powell et Emeric Pressburger, 1946, 1h 45mn

---

Exposition de photographies à l'UNESCO

Salle des Pas Perdus, Hall Miró, Espace Segur

Panorama du cinéma mondial
Exposition de photographies de films appartenant au patrimoine cinématographique des pays suivants : Allemagne, Argentine, Autriche, Australie, Bolivie, Brésil, Burkina Faso, Chili, Chine, Côte d'Ivoire, Danemark, Egypte, Equateur, Espagne, Estonie, Etats-Unis d'Amérique, Finlande, Grèce, Hongrie, Inde, Irlande, Israël, Italie, Japon, Lettonie, Liban, Ex-République yougoslave de Macédoine, Mali, Mexique, Niger, Norvège, Nouvelle-Zélande, Pérou, Portugal, République de Corée, République tchèque, Ukraine, Sénégal, Slovaquie, Slovénie, Suisse, Venezuela, Yougoslavie, Zaïre

Foyer de la Salle I
Aperçu de l'histoire des cinémas australien, britannique, français et suédois.

Salle des Actes
Exposition de dessins et marionnettes pour films d'animation (République tchèque).
Exposé sur la création et l'animation des marionnettes
Tous les jours à 14h30 et 17h30.

PRIDI BANOMYONG
(Luang Pradist Manudharm)
1900-1983

A Great Thai Commoner:
For Peace, Democracy
and Social Justice

CABINET RESOLUTION

Subject: The submission of Pridi Banomyong's name to the United Nations Educational, Scientific, and Cultural Organization (UNESCO) for its anniversaries of great personalities and historic events calendar.

The Cabinet officially sanctions the Ministry of Education's submission of Pridi Banomyong's name to UNESCO for its anniversaries of great personalities and historic events calendar. This official decision is also made pursuant to the centennial commemoration of Pridi Banomyong, the senior statesman, that is being held by the University of Moral and Political Science (Thammasat University). Pridi was the University's founder.

11 May 2000 will mark the centennial anniversary of Pridi. He had devoted the bulk of his life to the betterment of his country and society. Pridi had played a vital role in promoting and developing public awareness of issues of peace, democracy, and education. He was a moral conscience for the Thai people, and, more importanly, for humanity. Pridi stands tall as a sociopolitical icon. He had displayed, by any standards, considerable degree of honesty, loyalty, courage and sacrifice throughout his long career as Regent, Senior Statesman, Prime Minister, Minister of Interior, Minister of Foreign Affairs, Minister of Finance, and as the first Secretary General of Parliament. It is most appropriate that the Thai people look up to Pridi as a leading model.

Thai Cabinet meeting, 13 May 1997

Pridi Banomyong was one of the greatest Thais of this century. Great, that is, in strength of character, vision, achievement, and nobility of purposes. Like all great personalities in history, Pridi continues to live posthumously. Many of his ideas, because they are embedded in universal values, are still very relevant today, inspiring many in the younger generation. The Thais often find themselves returning to or rediscovering Pridi's ideas and vision of a better society, especially when they had initially rejected them.

THE UPBRINGING

Pridi Banomyong was born on 11 May 1900 in a boathouse off the southern bank of Muang Canal in Ayudhya, the former capital of Thailand. He was the eldest son of a relatively well to do farming family. At the age of 14, he completed his secondary education. Too young to enroll in any institution for higher education, Pridi stayed with his family for an extra two years, helping them in rice farming before darting off to law school in 1917. Two years later, he became a barrister-at-law and was simultaneously awarded a scholarship by the Ministry of Justice to study law in France. In 1924, he obtained his *"Bachelier en Droit"*, *"Licencié en Droit"* from *Université* de Caen and in 1926 a *"Doctorat d'Etat"* and *"Diplôme d'Etudes Supérieures d'Economie Politique"* from *Université* de Paris. Pridi was the first Thai to earn this appellation. In November 1928, a year after returning to Siam, Pridi married Miss Phoonsuk na Pombejra. They had six children.

THE BEGINNING OF A POLITICAL LIFE

In February 1927, while still in Paris, Pridi and six other Thai students and civil servants, later to become the core of the People's Party, held a historic meeting. They vowed to transform the Thai system of governance from absolute monarchy to a constitutional one. The group elected Pridi as their provisional leader. As their guiding stars, the People's Party laid down the so-called "Six Principles" to put Thailand on the road to spiritual and material progress:

108

Signing Ceremony with Minister Edwin Neville of U.S.A.
10 October 1937

Visiting Broadlands, England
September 1970
as invitedguests of Lord Louis Mountbattan

1. "To maintain absolute national independence in all aspects, including political, judicial, and economic;
2. To maintain national cohesion and security;
3. To promote economic well being by creating full employment and by launching a national economic plan;
4. To guarantee equality to all;
5. To grant complete liberty and freedom to the people, provided that this does not contradict the aforementioned principles; and
6. To provide education to the people."

Later in 1927, Pridi returned to Thailand and joined the Ministry of Justice where he served as judge and subsequently as assistant secretary to the Juridical Department. Meanwhile he found time to run a printing house where he published many law documents and books. He also became a lecturer at the Ministry's law school. However the hope for progressive sociopolitical and economic changes in Thailand never faded from Pridi's mind. The 1932 Revolution opened the avenue for Pridi to realize his vision of a better, more just society.

At dawn on 24 June 1932, the People's Party, consisting of government officials, military officers, and ordinary civilians rapidly and bloodlessly took control of the government, changing it from absolute to democratic, constitutional monarchy and installing the 1932 provisional constitution as the supreme law of the land. Pridi, the civilian leader of the People's Party, was the progenitor of this provisional constitution.

The 1932 provisional constitution served as a solid and fertile foundation for the growth and development of democracy in Thailand. It introduced two fundamental, hitherto unknown ingredients to Thai society and political culture: 1) the supreme power rests with all Siamese people; and 2) there must be a clear separation of legislative, executive, and judicial powers. Together, these two unprecedented principles brought about a complete transformation in the nation's power structure, planting the seeds of democracy in Thailand.

FOR PEACE, DEMOCRACY AND SOCIAL JUSTICE

Between 1933 and 1947 Pridi held many major political positions, including Minister of Interior, Minister of Foreign Affairs, Minister of Finance, Regent and Prime Minister. King Rama VIII officially appointed him "Senior Statesman" for life. Throughout these years as government official and leader, Pridi assiduously worked to realize the "Six Principles." Among his notable accomplishments, some of them having long-term impacts, are: the drafting of the nation's first economic plan; the founding of the University of Moral and Political Science (Thammasat University); the 1933 Municipality Act which allowed the people to elect their own local governments; the revocation of unequal treaties that Thailand had been forced to sign with foreign powers; the reformation of the unfair tax system; the compilation of the country's first revenue code; and the founding of what ultimately became the Bank of Thailand.

During the Second World War, once the Japanese had invaded and occupied Thailand, even as Regent, Pridi clandestinely led the Free Thai Movement to resist such action. In recognition of the brave cooperation and assistance rendered by this movment, the United States government subsequently recognized Thailand as an independent country that had been under Japanese military occupation as opposed to a belligerent state subject to postwar Allied control.

On 16 August 1945, at the advice of Lord Louis Mountbatten (the Allied South East Asia Commander), as Regent and Leader of the Free Thai Movment, Pridi declared null and void the Pibulsonggram Government's declaration of war on the Allied as it was against the will of the Thai people. Through the good work of the Free Thai Movement, Thailand had thus worked its passage to peace and pre-war status. Fifty years later, in 1995, the Thai cabinet gave belated recognition and declared 16 August the "Thai Peace Day".

Throughout these turbulent years, Pridi never lost sight of what 'democracy as a way of life' meant. He never tired of nurturing and protecting the infantile Thai democracy gurgling in its cradle. Unlike most of his genteel contemporaries, Pridi never related to the masses with distrust and trepidation. On the contrary, he had great faith in them. In the essay (1973) "Which Direction Should Thailand Take in the

Future," Pridi vividly and passionately reiterated his conception of participatory democracy, one that guided him all his life. He wrote, "Any system favoring a small section of a community will not last. In any community the majority must shape its future. [Here the majority includes] the deprived people, poor farmers, low-budget entrepreneurs, and patriotic capitalists who place the public interest above their own... and who want a new social system which provides a better living standard to the majority of people... social injustice [must be] abolished or reduced."

Pridi realized that a society is more democratic to the extent that fewer people are denied human rights and opportunities. He knew that political freedom without socioeconomic opportunities is a devil's gift. He tried to reduce and eventually to remove hierarchies of reward, status, and power in order to improve society. He wanted to foster solidarity and compassion among his compatriots, enabling them to develop themselves, come to care about, promote, and benefit from one another's well being as opposed to embarking on a cutthroat competition—a complete waste of energy. Pridi envisioned a society where all citizens helped contribute to the enrichment of the lives of all.

As Pridi neatly put it, "A society exists because of the participation of its members, and a social system which enables most people to legally influence decisions and move society forward is a democracy." He added that since every society has political, economic, social, and cultural dimensions, it is essential for a democratic society to not only promote political democracy but also "economic democracy" (e.g., fewer people are being denied economic opportunities) and democratic thinking (e.g., compassion).

For instance, to promote economic well being, Pridi advocated the creation of local cooperatives to undertake economic activities for the benefits of their members. The people should have direct control over their livelihood rather being dependent on the ruling circles' charity or philanthropy, he believed. Not infrequently, magnificent philanthropy masks brutal economic exploitation and charity becomes a pretext for maintaining laws and social practices which ought to be changed in the interest of justice and fair play, Pridi implied.

Pridi and his colleagues deemed it necessary for the people to fully understand the system of democratic governance and to be aware of their new rights and, hence, responsibilities under the newly-found system. As a result, in 1934 Pridi, then Minister of Interior, founded the University of Moral and Political Science. He was also appointed its first rector. The University was designed as an open institution offering numerous courses, including law, economics, human and social sciences. Reflecting his ideals, Pridi, in the speech made at the University's opening, declared "...A university is, figuratively, an oasis that quenches the thirst of those who are in pursuit of knowledge. The opportunity to acquire higher education rightly belongs to every citizen under the principle of freedom of education... Now that our country is governed by a democratic constitution, it is particularly essential to establish a university which will allow the people, and hence the public, to develop to their utmost capability. It will open up an opportunity for ordinary citizens to conveniently and freely acquire higher education for their own benefits and for the development of our country..." Indeed Thammasat University has been a leading institution in helping to promote and protect democracy in Thailand.

Pridi also firmly advocated international peace. As a minister in Field Marshal Pibulsonggram's government, Pridi consistently expressed his disagreement with the government's irredentism: the plan and aggression Thailand embarked on to reclaim former territories in Indochina from France while Paris was lying prostrate under German occupation during the Second World War. Another evidence worth citing is his effort to tell the international community the uselessness of international violence through the English-dubbed film he produced, *The King of the White Elephant*.

Not surprisingly, Pridi supported self-determination and independence for all colonial peoples. This was particularly apparent when he served as prime minister. Such a foreign policy was merely the international counterpart of his domestic, democratic reforms. After all, they attempted to empower the people, granting them with the essential freedoms and rights necessary to manage their own destiny. He even contemplated creating a South East Asian League (SEAL) among neighbouring nations.

Again, Pridi was the architect of the 1946 constitution, one of the most democratic in Thai history. The adoption of this constitution reflected the culmination of Pridi's relentless efforts to strive for social justice and establish a meaningful, as opposed to nominal, democracy in Thailand. The constitution guaranteed universal suffrage to both men and women and enabled the people to elect members of parliament in both the upper and lower houses. Human rights were well recognized and upheld in this constitution.

IN EXILE

On 9 June 1946, the young King Ananda Mahidol or Rama VIII was found mysteriously dead in his chamber with a bullet in his forehead. After visiting the palace and the scene and having consulted with leading members of the Royal Family, as prime minister, Pridi publicly declared this an "accident." Intending to undermine his popularity and power, Pridi's political opponent opportunistically trumpeted that the late King was murdered and that Pridi was involved in the regicide.

On the night of 8 November 1947, a group of military leaders and civilians staged a coup d'etat, using the regicide as one of the pretexts to destroy Pridi. (Numerous court decisions had since proven Pridi innocent.) Their tanks stormed Pridi's residence in Bangkok, forcing him to flee to Singapore. On 26 February 1949, Pridi, aided by a number of naval officers and Thais who favored a democratic government, unsuccessfully staged a counter-coup. Once again, he was banished from Thailand-this time never to return. Between 1949 and 1970, Pridi resided in China. He then lived an ordinary life joined by his wife and daughters in the suburb of Paris. There he died peacefully on 2 May 1983.

While in exile, he wrote profusely and gave numerous speeches, continuing to share with later generations his conceptions of democracy, peace and social justice. The seeds of democracy that Pridi planted in Thailand more than six decades ago are beginning to sprout. Whether or not his tree of liberty will continue to grow and branch out, to some extent, depends on how the Thais apply and learn from his vision.

For more information and donation, please contact:-
• Pridi Banomyong Foundation 65/1 Soi Thonglor, Wattana, Bangkok 10110
  Tel. 662 381-3860-1 Fax. 662 381-3859
  E-mail : pridi_institute@hotmail.com
• Committees on the Project for the National Celebration on the Occasion
  of the Centennial Anniversary of Pridi Banomyong, Senior Statesman
  (private sector) E-mail : pridi@ffc.or.th, www.pridi.or.th

Series to commemorate the centennial anniversary of the birth of Pridi Banomyong, Senior Statesman

THE KING OF THE WHITE ELEPHANT
by PRIDI BANOMYONG

Publisher :   Committees on the Project for the National Celebration
on the Occasion of the Centennial Anniversary of
Pridi Banomyong, Senior Statesman (private sector)
E-mail : Pridi@ffc.or.th   http://www.pridi.or.th
Project Chair - person : Sulak Sivaraksa
Committee Member and Secretary : Pibhop Dhongchai

Co-Publisher : Pridi Banomyong Institute
65/1 Soi Thonglor, Wattana, Bangkok 10110
Thailand (Siam)
Tel. 662 381-3860-1 Fax : 662 381-3859
E-mail : pridi_institute@hotmail.com

Producer : Project to produce media materials, for children
and youths, in honour of Pridi Banomyong,
Senior Statesman
Chairman : Pibhop Dhongchai
Editor : Santisukh Sopanasiri
Editorial Board : Karn Dhongchai, Prinat Apirat, Sudjai Bhomkoed

Co-Producer : Foundation for Children Publishing House
1845/328 Soi Charuslap, Sirindhorn Rd., Bangplud,
Bangkok, 10700 Thailand. (Siam)
Tel. (622) 881-1734 Fax : (662) 424-6280
E-mail:cpublish@ffc.or.th   http://www.ffc.or.th
Front cover design : Teerawat Mulvilai
Artwork : Papyrus Publication Co.,Ltd. Tel. 287-2492